"From its first assured sentence to its last,
Wyoming marks the debut of a gifted storyteller. This is
a compassionate novel, for all its violence and despair, an
authentic, pitch-perfect portrait of an America too often
caricatured or ignored. There are hard truths here, grit
and cruelty, but JP Gritton's fine prose is nuanced enough,
generous enough, to keep his troubled narrator's humanity,
his beating heart, apparent at every turn."

—ALICE McDERMOTT
author of *The Ninth Hour*

"Money, family, sex, crime, and mayhem—*Wyoming*
combines the thrill of genre work with the genuine human
investigation one hopes to see in a literary novel, and the
result is wickedly pleasurable and satisfyingly disturbing.
JP Gritton's terse prose about dark-minded men reminds
me of the novels of Pete Dexter. This is a marvelous
debut and a writer to watch."

—ROBERT BOSWELL
author of *Tumbledown*

Published by Tin House Books, Portland, Oregon

Distributed by W. W. Norton & Company

Library of Congress Cataloging-in-Publication Data

Names: Gritton, JP, 1984- author.
Title: Wyoming / JP Gritton.
Description: First U.S. edition. | Portland, Oregon : Tin House Books, 2019.
Identifiers: LCCN 2019013805 | ISBN 9781947793446 (pbk.)
Classification: LCC PS3607.R596 W96 2019 | DDC 813/.6—dc23
LC record available at https://lccn.loc.gov/2019013805

First U.S. Edition 2019
Printed in the USA
Interior design by Jakob Vala

www.tinhouse.com

WYOMING

JP GRITTON

TIN HOUSE BOOKS / Portland, Oregon

For John Lee

I

I'll tell you what happened and you can go ahead and decide. This was about a year ago, around when the Big Thompson went up. That fire made everybody crazy. A billboard out toward Montgrand reads: HE IS RISEN. And I wasn't ever the churchgoing type, but seeing fire wash down the mountain in a crazy-ass wave made me think twice about All That. Like maybe He's already here, and maybe you can read Him in flame and flood.

Day it started, my crew was working an addition for this guy Ronnie, lived up Left Hand Road. Now that was a job: big timber penning us in on all sides, keeping the sun off our backs. Around one in the afternoon, Ronnie would come a-prancing down the porch steps, big smile on his face. Then he'd get in his car and drive to town. Don't know what he did for a living, but it didn't look like he was working too hard. When Ronnie come back around five in the afternoon, we'd pack it in for the day. Sometimes he even brought us beer. He'd float downstairs, a case of Bud in his hand, grinning like jolly ole Saint Nick. He'd hand the beer out to everybody on the crew, that big smile on his face. Some kind of bonus, I guess. He always had a line of bullshit, like, Don't you gentlemen get sore, working all day like this? And you'd laugh, cause you

1

knew you had to. I didn't mind Ronnie. It was just he wanted poke so bad you could smell it on him.

Anyway, that was a good job. I made seven grand in three months, and I don't think I broke a sweat that whole time.

Then one morning the thunder come, loud enough to scare shit out of you. Great black clouds wash over the mountains and I turn around: "Get ready for a rain delay, boys!" and everybody laughs cause we all know this is about the downhillest contract we ever worked. But then I get this weird feeling. For one thing, it doesn't hardly rain. Then the lightning starts flaring. Then I see this bolt come down and just kiss the tree line.

We seen the red start in the brush by a hundred-year pine, and then we watched it creepy-crawl its way past bark and branches. Took about ten seconds for the fire to swallow that tree whole, and then it jumped, I swear to God, it jumped. And just like that it swallowed another great big pine. We must have looked like holy rollers at a revival: all slouching and slack-jawed, watching and waiting. I guess a minute went by before my best friend backslash brother-in-law, Mike Corliss, hollered, "Pack it up, fellas!"

So we did.

We got the chest onto the company truck and then we piled all the little stuff inside: skill saws and quick saws, pneumatics and drills. We had two compressors, a new one and an old one, and I hauled the new one into the back of my truck, I don't know why, I knew I had no cause to. But it was chaos by then: the whole time we're packing, we can see the fire chewing up the mountainside, coming right at us. It was raining a little, but near as I could tell it wasn't slowing the fire down any.

One by one, everybody takes off: Mike Corliss in the big F-250 marked LUNDEEN CONSTRUCTION LLC, then Tiny Tim and

Eric from Boston and Eric from Phoenix, then the Mexicans. I don't know why I didn't haul ass out of there. I don't know why I just stood in the lot, looking around, trying to think of what we forgot. Then it hits me that nobody's told Ronnie.

So I hustle up the stairs, fast as I can, and when I get up to the door I pound on it like crazy. I guess the fire was about a mile off, maybe more, but it seemed closer. Maybe I imagined it, but I could feel the heat against my face. When he opened the door, he was in a pair of jogging shorts and a tank top, all barefoot and sweaty. I don't know what he was doing in there and I sure as hell don't want to. I pointed west. I told him, "Get your ass out of here!" Motherfucker just looks at me. I can see "White Trash" ticker-taping over his eyes.

"Fire!" I shout, and I'll be goddamned if I can't help smiling. "Fire, you dipshit!"

Kind of seems like the Big Thompson going up was the beginning of the bad times for me and Mike. First of all, the work dried up. You'd think all them houses burning would mean a lot of building. Well it didn't. Now they were gone, wasn't anybody wanted to build up there. Plain scared, must've been. We did a reno out in Erie, we built a rich lady's deck in Boulder. That's about it.

By the time the boss man—Jake Lundeen, I mean—called me in, I hadn't had steady work in a month and a half. That was the first time I ever been in his trailer. Only reason to go in there is Lundeen wants to chew you out or you're picking up your paycheck. Account of he was my best friend, Mike Corliss picked up my paychecks for me, and I never gave Lundeen no reason to chew me out.

It was about the kind of office you might expect a guy like Lundeen to have: had his contractor's license from the State of

Colorado framed and hung on the wall, alongside photographs
of himself looking cut in jungle fatigues, smiling with some other
dudes. He had his POW/MIA flag in the far corner, next to a steel
shelf where the company's books were lined up, each with a year
wrote down the side in yellow: 1975, 1976, 1977, all the way up
to 1987. Apart from that, I remember he kept some Indian shit
in there. A little guy with a mohawk playing a flute etched into a
hunk of flagstone. Drums. Eagle feathers. He had a piece of raw-
hide about the shape and size of a dinner plate, strung up with
rabbit fur and feathers and beads.

"Dream catcher," he told me when I asked him what it was.
"Keeps all the bad dreams out. Anyway, it's supposed to."

"I need one," I said. I don't know why. Pretty much right away
I wished I hadn't. I was nervous as all hell. When I'm nervous, I
talk foolish.

"Well I guess we all need one," he said after a while. "How you
doing, Shell?"

I said I was all right. I said I wished to hell the work wasn't so
slow. See what I mean? Foolish.

"It's about to get a whole lot slower," he said. "It'll be winter
soon. Actually."

He give me this look.

"That's kind of what I want to talk to you about," he said. "Cause
it's been awfully slow. And when the work's slow, the money's slow.
And when the money's slow, people will sometimes get dumb ideas
that seem like good ones."

I nodded, to show him I got his drift.

"I'm not singling you out," he said. "I'm not accusing. But
there's a few things gone missing."

"Like what?"

"There's a bunch of little stuff," he said. "I'm not worried about the little stuff. But there's one big thing I am sort of worried about."

I asked him, "What's missing?"

"We seem to have had an air compressor simply vanish. Into thin air."

Now he'd said it, I didn't feel half so nervous anymore.

"Which one?" I asked. "We got a few."

"Not 'we,'" he said. "I. I have a few."

He figured he could flush me out, but he was dead wrong. I didn't say anything at first, then I decided I'd cut right to the chase: "I guess you think I did it."

"I never said that. I'm talking to everybody."

"Well I don't know about it," I said. "Maybe it went in the fire."

"I thought about that," he said. "It's possible. But I doubt it."

I didn't ask him why he doubted it. I said, "You asked Hector and Luis?"

"I know Hector and Luis," he told me. "I don't know you very well."

"So you think I must of did it."

He put his hands up and said he never said that. Then we were quiet. I looked around his office, waiting for Lundeen to tell me I could go. I looked at the picture of him in the army. Even in Vietnam, the dude seemed like he'd never had to worry about anything.

"I don't know you very well, Shelley," he said, "but I do know Mike, and I know that it hasn't been an easy time for you, this past while."

Momma, I figured he was meaning. Or Lij, maybe, and the hundred twenty acres he lost on his deathbed. Either way, I wasn't about to bite on that one in a million years.

5

"Anyway," Lundeen went on after a good long quiet spell, "I'm not accusing anybody: just saying that I could see how it might seem like a good idea, even though it was a bad idea, to take something that belongs to me. I could understand it, I think. And if the guy who did it returned the air compressor to me, then I could probably see my way to not getting the police involved."

Time kind of stumbled along.

"Cause the thing is," he said, "it'd take me hardly any time to figure it out. Tell you what I'd do. I'd take a day off. I'd go to every pawnshop between the Springs and Fort Collins. I'd ask to see their air compressors, and then when I found mine, I'd ask to see the pawn slip."

It was about the dumbest thing I'd ever heard. If he checked every pawnshop from Fort Collins to the Springs, he still wouldn't find the fucking thing. I knew cause, maybe a week earlier, I'd got a little drunk and made up my mind to drive to Devils Tower. But that's a hell of a long drive. I got as far as Cheyenne and hawked the air compressor there. Five hundred bucks. It was almost all gone.

Wish I could help you, I kept telling Lundeen. Maybe I overdid it. I guess it doesn't matter: he knew I'd ripped it. It's like he said: he trusted the other guys on the crew, but he didn't trust me. When I walked outside, there was cold in the air, and I wondered what I'd do about supper.

Well it's hard working for a man when he's pretty much looked you in the eye and called you a thief. I wasn't ever quite fired, and I didn't exactly quit, either. I just sort of dipped out, if you read me. Never told nobody I was doing it, just quit going. It must've been Mike told my brother about the situation. That fat bastard come swinging through the front door, didn't even knock. It was cool out, but apart from sweats he didn't wear anything but a tee shirt, and in just that he was still panting and red in the face.

"You run here?" I said, just like always. I didn't even get up to shake his hand. From the couch I watched him do his Godzilla march over to the easy chair I kept in the corner. It was leather with three settings (sitting, laying, reclining), and the truth is I hardly set in the fucking thing. I don't know how to explain how come I didn't, except to say I never felt clean enough. When Clay set down, the chair groaned like a church organ.

"Heard about Lundeen's," he said.

I said, "Yeah, well."

"How you holding up?"

"Oh," I said, "you know."

I should've told him scram, but now he was here I figured hell with it. I even went and got him something to drink out of the fridge.

"You got no Pepsi?" he said when I handed him Coke. It was like him to razz me when he hasn't been in the house but five minutes.

"There's Pepsi down the road," I said, meaning the 7-Eleven on Main. "You want Pepsi, go there."

He said, "No use us fighting already."

I thought about getting one last dig in, but on the whole I figured Clay was right: there was no point.

"Anyway," I said. "I'm okay. Had a little scratch saved up."

He smiled: "I bet you did."

I guessed he must mean the compressor. Well, fine. If that's what he thought, let him think it. Still, I figured it wasn't any of his damn business.

I don't know what it is, I just can't concentrate when my brother is in a room. The TV was on, but my brain didn't know what my eyes saw on the screen. It was all of it just shapes and colors, twisting on the glass like ghost acrobats. My whole life was passing me by.

"I guess I'll get something together for the winter," I told him.

"Something like what?" he wanted to know.

Which is when I smelled a rat. It wasn't like my brother to wonder. Matter of fact, it wasn't like my brother to come to me like this at all. Tigers don't change their stripes, neither do jailbirds. I could see his, plain enough.

"Don't worry about it," I told him, getting sulky. "I'll find something."

We watched the TV awhile. Then I guess Clay must've got tired of beating around the bush.

"I come here as a favor."

"No favor to me," I told him. "Tell me what you want before you break that chair."

He didn't say anything for a second. Then he said, "I didn't mean you. May told me to come."

May, he said. Our sister. Which was a load of bullshit.

"We heard about your trouble, is all," he said. "Kind of figured you could use some help."

I just about messed myself, laughing. Help, my ass.

Anyway Clay didn't stay much longer, a half hour or so. Just enough to catch his breath, I guess. The TV thundered: pure noise. When he stood up finally, he didn't say goodbye. He walked right on out the door. When he'd gone, I stood up and turned the deadbolt.

The day I went to visit Mike, this was toward end of November, the whole house stunk like what was coming. I forgot to tell you that Mike's little girl had got sick in the summer. I don't like children, but I almost liked Layla. She was a quiet thing, but not so quiet she made you nervous. She looked a lot like Mike, matter of fact: golden-haired, with big blue eyes and a sad mouth. I guess it was about a couple months earlier they'd figured out she was about rot-through with cancer.

That girl was bad sick. Just this stumpy little skeleton, and the sheets pulled up to her chest. It did something to me, seeing her fingers that were just like matchsticks, and her eyes set deep in bruisey sockets, and what was left of her hair all damp and twisty on her forehead.

May set there next to her on the bed. My voice was gone and she had to tell me, "Say hello to your niece."

I said, "Hi, Layla."

She was a polite girl but she didn't make no move, not even a tilt of her head, to show she'd heard me. Veins ran crooked in her skinny neck. She watched me standing in the doorframe, thinking whatever she thought. Fuck all. I wondered does she know I'm a bad man.

May bent to the girl, whispered soft: "Say, Hi Uncle Shell, Layla."

The girl lifted her hand. She had no voice to speak to me. And maybe if she had, she still wouldn't have said anything. I don't blame her. The poison they ran into her veins made her weak: cure's worse than the disease, like they say. But then again the disease seemed pretty god-awful.

"I just come to say hello to your daddy," I told her.

Them two on the bed seemed to wait. They must want me to leave, I thought, but I couldn't. I just stared at that kid, into the blue-black eyes where her life was fading and flickering like a bum lightbulb. Even if she looked half-dead, you could still see how much Layla favored Mike. And the thought went through me like a blade: I got to do something about this.

"She's a little angel," I said.

"She sure is," said May, and she almost smiled. I didn't get any kind of pleasure from watching May suffer like that, I'll tell you. I was grateful to her when she let me go, nodding her head at the door:

"Mike's out in back," she said.

I went through the den, where old magazines had been stacked into crushing towers, and the radio played so low that all you could hear was a slanty buzz. I pulled the black doorknob and stepped back into the cold I'd just come from. Them days, Mike and May lived out past the Montgrand city limits. They'd got a nice place, bought when the land was still cheap: about two acres, and the Saint Vrain Creek run right through it.

Mike was a ways off, at the edge of the property, setting on the cutting stump and smoking. He had a pushcart and in the pushcart there was some firewood. I guess he must have heard me coming through the door, but he didn't turn around when it shut.

"Hey," I called. Still he didn't turn around. My guts sunk when I thought he might be having himself a cry. Nobody could fault him for that. I sure as hell wouldn't. I slowed up my pace a little, I guess to give him a chance to get himself together. But when he stood up and turned to me, his eyes were dry.

"That chimney's got something wrong with it," he said. "Gets smoky as hell in there."

"Seemed all right to me," I said.

"That's cause May put the electric on."

I nodded.

"It's like living in a muffler. That kid, like she ain't got enough problems." Mike was quiet for a while. Then he said, "This is a bad deal here."

"It sure is," I told him. "Y'all can stay with me, you don't like the smoke."

I meant my place down on Hover, Mrs. Gamliel's building. It was real cheap account of I did the mowing sometimes, and the gutters and things like that. Besides that, Mrs. Gamliel likes me. There was gas heat and plenty of space there. Layla and her momma could stay in my room. Me and Mike could camp out on the living room floor.

"Thanks," Mike said, "but I guess we better leave Lay be."

Probably he was right about that. I thought about her waving at me. I said, "How are you all fixed?"

Mike said, "What do you mean?"

I said, "For cash."

He give me a funny look: "That an offer?" he said, and I knew what he meant. He meant: What happened to the air compressor?

By now Mike had been working for Jake Lundeen since him and May and Layla come out to Colorado, back in '85. Since it was Mike got me the job there, I knew I had put him in a jackpot. I didn't like it, but that was how it was. When I didn't talk, he said, "Anyway, we're all right. I had some savings, so did May." Then after a while, he goes on, like it isn't any kind of big deal: "Clay's been helping some."

Boy, it spread through me like wildfire. I couldn't keep my voice straight cause I felt like I was choking.

"He's been what now?"

"He's helped us some," Mike said. "We've got a hundred-dollar copay every time we go in that fucking place. Clay pays."

"He pays for the hospital?" I said.

"And other stuff."

Turned out Clay gave them money for all kinds of things: helped with the groceries and the electric, a down coat for Layla.

I said, "I don't know where to hell he gets the money."

It was a dumb thing to say, considering, and I guess Mike couldn't help smiling at me. We were quiet, and then he said, "You better bring it back, Shelley."

I said, "Bring what back?"

When he quit smiling, he looked as awful as I felt right then.

"All right," he told me, "your funeral."

I stood out there with my friend Mike Corliss, watching him chop the wood slow and steady. He pulled the axe over his head. He drove the bright edge into the heart of the wood. The kindling fell around the stump with a clatter, and I stooped to gather it into the pushcart.

While we worked I thought about Clay, wondering what his game was. On the face of it, he was helping Mike. But I knew Clay too well, and I knew help from Clay was no help at all.

"When's he want the money back?" I asked.

Mike set a big white block of wood up on the stump, drew up the blade, halved it.

"I don't think it's a loan," he said. "I think he just means it as a kindness."

And it didn't sound right: didn't sound much like Clay, anyway. Maybe he didn't want anything now, but that didn't mean he would want nothing later. It was a loan, even if Mike didn't know it was. And the devil was to pay.

"Come on," Mike said when we'd done. "You ready?"

I piled the last bit of the kindling into the cart and we headed on in. We were busy for a while piling the firewood against the wall of the house, where Mike had a strip of plywood cantilevered against the wet. It was good work, I could see that. When we'd got through, we took a few of the bigger wood blocks and went inside.

In the house I could hear the girl's voice all soft and crumpled-sounding: "I'm not thirsty," she kept saying. "I don't want it." She would die soon and everyone knew she would die and Clay was liable to come out the better for it. Drove me crazy, thinking about it.

After we'd set the wood against the claws of the stove, Mike walked to the kitchen and pour his little girl a glass of water. I followed him.

"Set on down there," he said, poking his chin at the red Formica table him and May'd brought with them from Missouri. I did. With the glass of water in his hand he made for his little girl's room. I just set there, listening. I could hear their voices, low. May laughed and then I heard Mike laughing, too. Maybe the girl was laughing, but I couldn't tell.

When Mike come back to the kitchen I asked, "What were y'all carrying on about?"

"Nothing," he said, quick, so I wondered maybe were they laughing at me. It made me feel silly, and shy, like a kid hanging out with grown-ups. I didn't appreciate it much.

I said, "You needed help, you should've come to me."

We were quiet. I thought about them laughing in the next room. I wanted a drink bad but it was not the time for it. One of these days, it's all going to make sense. Just then, though, Mike wasn't helping things.

"How can you hate him so much?" he asked.

And before I could think of a way around it, I said, "How can you not?"

"Cause he's May's brother," Mike told me. "And cause family's all you got, when it comes down to it."

You're all I got, I almost told him, but I knew it wouldn't sound right. He looked so tired all of a sudden. Some reason, I felt like

13

apologizing to him: it was like I was the one who'd brought all this
down on them. I knew it was crazy. I was Mike's best friend. All the
wickedness in the world wouldn't change that.

"Don't you know where that money come from?" I said, when
I couldn't think of what else to say.

Mike just shook his head, like he couldn't believe my nerve.

"You can ask him yourself when he gets here," he told me,
standing up and making for Layla's room. "Clay and the girls are
coming for supper."

I wouldn't've stayed but that Clay and me had business.

Back in '72, a while before I come out West, Clay married himself a piece of redheaded Arkansas trash named Nancy, and then
Nancy had two girls by Clay named Erin and Aileen. Them girls
were redheaded trash just like their momma and you could see a
reckless future playing out when you looked them in the eye. The
one called Erin already had tits even if she was just twelve that
year. Aileen was ten but she had as foul a mouth as you ever heard.
She was prettier than her sister, and knew it.

When they showed up, the dark was already edging in on the
plains. They walked in and seen me setting at the kitchen table,
and I heard that little bitch Aileen mutter, "Oh, shit."

Clay had on a jean jacket over his tee shirt, and a pair of sweats.
I'm pretty sure they were the same sweats he wore when he come
to see me that day in October. I told him, "Guess the whole family
don't bother with knocking."

Nancy laughed and stooped down to kiss my cheek: "Family
don't have to knock," she said. "How you doing, Shelley?"

I don't know, I guess Nancy's all right: a good woman, even
if she is trash. She's sick, too, a little, though just at the moment I

can't remember what the sickness is called, and she doesn't ever complain. In fact you'd hardly notice but that some days she moves slower than others, and kind of jerking and jittering around some, like an old dog.

"I'm all right," I said, but I wasn't fooling anybody. Truth is, I couldn't stop thinking about Clay trying to get my best friend Mike Corliss over a barrel.

"You look like you just sucked a lemon," said Nancy. Her girls smirked.

When Mike come in he put on a brave face: smiled and kissed Nancy and hugged Clay like the brother he sure as hell wasn't. When he scooped up Erin and Aileen, you could tell by the way they looked at Mike they were kind of sweet on him.

"May'll be out in a second," he said. "Layla had a accident."

"Poor little bug," said Nancy.

We were all quiet for a while, and then Mike wondered if burgers sounded all right to everybody. He fetched a package of ground beef from the fridge and set it in the sink. He turned to the girls and asked were they hungry now, and even though they shook their heads he fetched down some potato chips from the cupboard and opened them up. That's just like Mike: trying to make everybody happy.

"How's she doing?" Nancy wondered, while her girls laid into the chips.

"She's all right," Mike said. "We won't know much until next month. That's when we see the oncologist. They got to see how everything's going."

"We'll be praying for you," said Nancy.

Mike didn't say anything. I thought maybe he's thinking it won't do no good and I thought maybe he's right to think it.

It was a solemn-type moment, quiet but for the girls sucking down them potato chips. I stared hard at the one called Erin. I said, "You keep on eating like that, you're liable to end up like your daddy."

Don't think I'm proud of what I said, cause I'm not. Matter of fact, I felt sorry as hell for saying it. The room gone real quiet. Erin got this worn-out look on her face. Then Mike smiled at her and said she ought to have just as much as she wanted, cause we weren't liable to eat for another hour or so.

I don't know what to tell you: I have what you'd call a mean streak.

When May had finished cleaning up Layla's bedsheets, she come out and hugged everybody and they set around and visited in the den. Nobody talked to me or asked me anything, which I didn't mind. I guess Layla must've been sound asleep in the next room, cause she didn't make a peep that whole time.

"It'll be mighty slow this winter," Mike said, shaking his head. "Slump got everybody scared."

"I'll tell you who isn't hurting," Clay said. "The boss man. He isn't hurting one bit."

Mike shrugged: "Lundeen's fair."

"Fair, shit," Clay said. "Get your contractor's license. Then you'll see what's fair."

Never mind he didn't know the first fucking thing about it.

"I don't have time to study," Mike told him. "And that test cost money."

Clay said, "If it's the money, don't worry about it."

That was about as much as I could take. I stood up. I said, "Come on outside."

For a second Clay looked like he didn't aim to follow. Four years earlier, after he got out of Huntsville, maybe he wouldn't have. But I was big now, and strong from the work. I guess he didn't want to see what would happen if he stayed put. After a minute he got his ass off the couch and follow me outside.

I walked down to the woodpile and the axe face-first in the cutting stump. In the way-off I could see where the mountains reared up into great purple piles, and before that the fields of splintered corn and winter wheat the yellow of old teeth. My breath was a ghost in the hard blue air. I watched Clay come. He was panting and drawing the collar of his jacket up around his wattle. I didn't want any part of this. I didn't want anything to do with him. And still I said: "Well go on and tell me about it."

Before he answered me, he took a roach out of the pocket of his jacket and lit up. Took this big old drag: "Tell you about what?"

I might've figured he'd play dumb. I said, "Tell me about this job you've got."

He looked at me, the roach flaring red. I watched the smoke floating east on the cold wind, headed for night. He said, "Two thousand dollars."

I said, "That isn't much."

He said, "It's plenty for what you'll be doing."

I said, "What is it you think I'm going to do?"

He said, "Drive to Houston."

And I said, "What's in the car?"

And he said, "What do you think?"

And I just laughed at him: "Favor, my ass," I told him.

Well there we were. Two thousand dollars to run his weight. Okeydokey, forget it. I said, "You can kiss my ass, Clay."

He did not appreciate that. He said, "I'm trying to help you. It's either you do it or I find somebody else to do it. And it won't be hard to find somebody else."

He puffed away and I saw meanness at the corners of his eyes. He sort of chuckled to himself. He said, "Hell, I bet Mike'd do it. Sort of sounds like he could use the work, too."

I seen what he meant clear enough. He meant the groceries and the electric, a down coat for Layla. He meant: Mike'd just about do it for free if I asked him, wouldn't he? I'll tell you right now, I wanted to swing that axe at him. I wanted to bring the bright edge hard against his goddamn neck. I might have picked it up and did it, but to tell the truth I seen this coming. After a while I just said, "What gets to me is you don't even know how evil you are."

He looked at me. And I thought to myself, No: he knows damn well. After a second I said, "All right. But I want three thousand."

He said, "Twenty-five."

"Okay," I told him, "but I need five hundred up front."

After something like that I couldn't abide staying for dinner. I walked around the far side of the house, past the garage, so they wouldn't spy me from the den. When I come around the edge of the garage, though, May seen me from the kitchen. She had the window open to let the grease smoke out and she called to me, stooping under the glass.

I went over and nodded at her. I said I couldn't stay.

She watched me for a second before she spoke. Quiet like that, she looked just like Momma. She said, "You and Clayton are at it again."

It wasn't any kind of question, so I just shrugged.

"Are you going to do it?" she asked.

I played dumb, I don't know why: "Do what?" I said.

"Clay might have some work for you, is what I heard."

She drew up her shoulders, turned her eyes away from me.

"Yeah," I said, deciding there wasn't any harm in them knowing. "I'm going to do it."

Something soft and cold fell on my cheek. I looked up and saw the snow had started. Its smell in the air was heavy, like an animal's.

"Wait a second," she said. I watched her go to the counter and take out a bun and scoop one of the hamburgers onto it. Then she reached out and give me the hamburger, the grease still running down the side. My stomach growled when I smelled it. I said thank you, and then I walked to my truck and drove off.

It snowed fourteen inches that night, but by the morning they had I-25 cleared pretty good. I made Cheyenne in just about an hour. I always expect Wyoming to feel different, but it never does. When I got to the pawnshop and lay the ticket on the counter, the dude just squinted at me for a second. He said, Didn't expect to see you again. Yeah, I told him, me neither. After a minute he hauled the air compressor from where he had kept it in the window with an $800 price tag and set it down next to the counter. I took Clay's five hundred dollars from my wallet and handed it to him, then I picked up the air compressor and walked out the door. I didn't even look back, that's how mean I was feeling.

Somehow it seemed longer, going south.

Lundeen's car was out front, by the trailer. He drives a 1983 Lincoln Mark VII with tuck-and-roll upholstery and a cobalt-and-silver paint job. It give me a funny feeling to park right next to him. Opening the gate, I said out loud to nobody or everybody: "I'm never going to have to do this again."

That compressor weighed about three tons. I guessed that's what it was like, being Clay: like having a great big stone hanging round your neck. I humped that thing across the lot, up the rickety two-by-four stairs. Don't think I bothered with knocking.

Lundeen was at the desk, all his books and papers around him. Just judging by his face, I don't think he was all that surprised to see me. I set the compressor down on the floor, and then I turned round and walked out.

I must've been halfway to my truck when I heard him come out the door of his trailer: "Hey!" he called. "Wait a sec."

Something about his voice made me stop and turn and wonder. He waved me back up the stairs. He said, "Cold out here."

I wasn't afraid. I did not even feel ashamed, all of a sudden. I walked up the steps and back into the office. He didn't try making small talk, which I appreciated. Next to the desk where his papers were, he had a blower going. I just stood in the warm, waiting. From the top of that steel bookshelf, he took down one of the books. When he opened it I could see that inside were checks, three to a page. He was busy a while, deciding how much to give me, and then writing it down.

"What were you getting here?"

"Thirteen," I said.

"Lucky thirteen," he said. Then he tore the check loose and walked over and handed it to me. Six hundred sixty-six dollars, made out to Shelley Cooper. The memo read SEVERANCE PAY. You had to hand it to the guy, he had a sense of humor. I couldn't help it. I smiled.

Walking to my truck, I told myself I'd never cash it. Driving home, I told myself I couldn't afford not to.

Three weeks later, I drove to Texas with Clay's dope.

Night before I left, I went to that site up Left Hand Road, Ronnie's place. I don't know how to explain to you why I went there, but it pulled me like the current of a river. Like one minute I'm turning the keys in my ignition and the next minute my headlights are carving the gravel out of the dark, and my hands are twisting the wheel. After the fire, that big old house was nothing but a patch of concrete and a couple black logs laid one on top of the other. The add-on was just gone, so were all the trees: fire plucked that mountain like a chicken. He Is Risen: See what I mean? Sometimes you'll get an idea of the size of things.

With the car still going and the headlights on, I walked around the lot. I had my work boots on and I didn't care if they got dirty. The snow had melted by then, but the ash must have been an inch deep. Unbelievable.

I got to wondering whatever happened to old Ronnie.

Last I seen him, he was standing outside his car, watching the flame coming: I don't believe he knew whether to leave or stay. I wondered did he have insurance. I wondered did he land on his feet. I thought about how funny it would look, him driving up right then, finding me at the spot where his house used to be. I couldn't think of what I'd say to him. Sorry about all this.

Nobody ever come, though.

For a while I stood there, watching the snow make stardust in my headlights. Then I got in my truck and drove back to town.

II

I made pretty good time, getting down to Texas. Took I-25 south, on into New Mexico for a stretch, then east through Dalhart and Amarillo, where there was roadwork and the cars and cowboy trucks and semitrucks creaking along while the sun went piss-yellow and dripped down my rearview mirror. By the time that crew waved me on, it was full dark and my hands fixed so tight to the wheel it was hard to let go. My legs just screaming. I went through Dallas, this great big Technicolor spike in the night. Past Dallas come a whole bunch of places you never heard of. Fairfield, Buffalo, Centerville, Leona. I went straight through Huntsville, where Clay served five years on an eight-year sentence for possession with intent. I got to Houston right when the sun come up, this evil red above the tangle of steel and glass. Swear to God, it almost looked pretty.

I guess it was about seven in the morning I pulled off the highway, about the first place I could find. This hotel wasn't the rattiest little fleabit shithole in Houston, I don't guess, but probably it would've been close. Three two-story buildings with cracks in the vinyl siding black as black mold made a great big U round a parking lot

23

where weeds big and sprawly as live oak were rearing out of the asphalt. Manager's office was a little bungalow off to one end.

THE SEASIDE, read the peeled decal in the window there. Which is funny, cause there isn't any sea in Houston, just this saltwater bog they cut crossed thirty miles of nothing. I had made out the canal from the highway, past silos and train yards and the bowed-out shells of diesel containers. I've never saw the ocean, not once in my life, and that's what I was trying to picture when I walked through the clattery door and saw my best friend Michael Corliss just standing there behind the front desk.

Broad-shouldered, that sheen to his skin of a man accustomed to doing work out of doors. Same blue-jay-blue eyes, same sad mouth. Twins, you might've thought, but then after a beat you noticed the nose was a little wider than Mike's, and the eyes set at a different angle, and the hair a color more like dishwater than gold. Still I had to pause there a minute, blinking: that's how much the hotel clerk put me in mind of Mike. Even the way he talked was the same.

"Whoa, buddy," he called. "Look like you just saw a ghost."

And I guess it was true, guess I must've looked pretty rough. My body felt like one big pulled muscle.

"Had yourself a drive, huh?" he said, and they were Mike's eyes telling me to get it off my chest. But I didn't, I wouldn't. I knew better than to run my mouth to some hotel clerk. Where was I coming from, he wanted to know, and was the weather up in Dallas bad as they said it was on the news, and what business brung me to Houston. I knew he was just being friendly, but all the same I didn't care much for friendliness right then. I'd come for work, I told him, said I was driving in from Missouri—plates on my truck still read Missouri—and I said I wanted the daily rate, not the weekly, account of I would just be here the one day.

"Working on Christmas Eve?"

"Pretty much."

He wanted to know what line of work I was in, and I said, "Oil."

And this hotel clerk nodded like he knew something about it and asked what outfit.

"Claymore-Union Extraction Services" is what I said, like a prayer I had memorized, but the clerk give me a curious sort of look and it crossed my mind I had said the wrong thing. I can see now that maybe this is how a suspicious feeling got started between us, but in the end he just nodded his head.

"Twelve years, almost," he said. "That's for how long I was out in them fields. How I did this."

He held up his hand, which after a second I could see wasn't his hand at all. It was painted a paler shade than the rest of him, and it was stiff and plastic-looking besides, a mannequin's hand.

"Mousehole," he said. "Pipe come up right against the brace, 'cept my hand was in the way. Settlement money's how we bought this hotel."

Dang, I told him. But in my head I was cursing myself for a fool. Roughnecking, me? Who doesn't know a goddamned thing about it. I can't think of why I didn't just tell him the truth, or half of it, which was that I worked in construction. You'd better be more careful, I told myself, if you mean to get out of this all right.

Now the hotel clerk reached with his good hand to fetch a set of keys from the metal cabinet where they kept them.

"Believe it or not, I used to be a southpaw," he said.

Which give me a strange feeling in my bones, account of my best friend Michael Corliss is a lefty, too. Now the clerk held the keys up and kind of jangled them.

"Had to learn it all over again," he said. "Writing my name, hold a fork, everything. Tell you, I still have dreams about it. I'm stood over the line and I got the torch up, and then it hits me I don't have any mask on . . ."

He carried on that way, and I knew I was supposed to wag my head and give this fellow some line of bullshit like, gee, that sounds like a rough trail. And I would've, he was easy enough to like, but for the dope in my truck.

Besides that, I had the feeling he was testing me. Trying me out. Real casual he went: "You mind signing the registry?"

With the keys yet in his hand, he reached and took an old split-up leather-bound book from under the desk—I figured he must keep a shotgun down there, too, likely as not—and handed me a pen.

MICHAEL EDWARD CORLISS, I wrote, MONTGRAND, MISSOURI.

When I'd done writing, he smiled at the name a second, snapped the book shut. I followed him through the door and outside, and he went on in a puzzled-sounding voice:

"Claymore-Union, you said?"

"Claymore-Union Extraction Services."

"Huh," he said. Just huh.

We passed one, two, three doors, and I half listened while he told me there was no smoking allowed, and how if I want to smoke I'd better use the ashtray cause there's an additional fee for damage to the carpet, et cetera and so on.

Room four, we passed, five, six . . .

There'd be no trouble, I told him. Didn't smoke and didn't intend on having any guests, either.

"Well mind you don't," he said. "Me, you don't have to worry about. But Carlie, that's my wife, you don't want to mess with her."

He laughed, then went serious again: "Her brother, neither. Clint, that's the night manager. Now you'll want to steer clear of him altogether."

But by then I'd pretty much quit paying attention to him, account of the clerk was drawing up on the door to my room. Which was room number eleven.

And I should explain to you: I don't like the number. I am not superstitious about this sort of thing, not usually, but circumstance has a way of driving you out of your mind. Like for example, Momma died on August eleven, 1978. And May eleven, four years later, was the day Syrena left with our son. The day they let Clay out of Huntsville? Try January eleven, 1983. And it occurs to me now, what all I'm relating to you took place exactly one week before the first of the year, 1988, and eighty-eight is eleven, eight times. So you see, I have what you'd call a history with the number. And what I was thinking to myself, while the hotel clerk fit the key in the lock: this is a strange omen here.

Never mind it was about the ugliest fucking hotel room you ever saw. Curtains were brown and the wooly carpet looked like it needed cleaned, and it was the same mothy gray as the bedspread. There was a little brown desk next one of the little gray beds, a little brown lamp set upon it. We are talking a hotel room out of East Germany here, but that isn't why I didn't like it. I didn't like it cause this was room number eleven and eleven is an unlucky number and I needed all the luck I could get.

"You got another room I could have?"

The look on his face, you'd think I just pissed on his shoes. So I explained I wanted something just a little bigger, that I might like to spread out some. And hell, I could've afforded the Ritz-Carlton, thanks to Jake Lundeen's check.

"Mr. Corliss," he said, "the honeymoon suite is occupied."

27

I nodded, I just about made up my mind to let it go. But then I told him, "Just the same, friend, I'd like another room."

"They all look like this. They're all this exact size."

He was smiling a little, studying me as he did it. I told him yes, I understand, not wanting to explain but not quite seeing a way round it. I scratched at the back of my head.

"Please," I told him, "I'd sure appreciate it."

"There something the matter with this room, Mr. Corliss?" he wanted to know. "We're booked solid until the New Year, you pretty much got the last room. Only other room available is fourteen, which—"

But I bulldozed what he was about to say: "Fourteen's fine," I said. "Fourteen'll do her."

"And room fourteen, like I was saying to you, the television been broke in fourteen."

"It's all right about the TV," I told him. "I don't mind." And as a matter of fact I didn't. I wasn't planning to do much but sleep until I went to drop off Clay's dope. I said, "I'll take fourteen, thank you."

And the clerk took him a deep breath, kind of looking round the room for whatever I didn't like about the place. Finally he put his head back and laughed, said, "You're a particular kind of fellow, Mr. Corliss, aren't you?"

And he had a laugh just like Mike's. And it's like I told you, he was an all right fellow, just it give me a strange feeling to talk to him.

When he'd fetched the keys, the hotel manager showed me inside room fourteen, which was just like he'd said: same brown curtains drawed crossed the windows, same mothy carpet and bed linens to match, same little desk set off in the corner. The only difference was the TV on the bureau. The back panel was off on this one, and the red and blue and yellow wires was all spilled out behind. A heavy-looking toolbox set open on the floor, and now the manager kicked at it with the toe of his work boots: "Repairs in progress, as they say."

And he stood there, his arms folded over his chest, and he give me the same rap he'd gave me about room eleven: use a ashtray, don't have no guests, steer clear of this Clint fellow, the night manager, et cetera and so on.

Then he stopped talking of a sudden: "You sure you don't mind about this TV set?"

No, I said, I didn't mind.

Waving with the mannequin hand over to the TV, he says, "You want to know something? That thing been busted for about two months now. That's how long I've been trying to fix it. Carlene, that's my wife, she says better we get a new one. One of these days, we'll have a no vacancy and somebody want a room with a TV in it, it's liable to cost us money. But I'm too stubborn. I'm trying to fix this thing two months. What do you make of that?"

I shrugged. I didn't make much of anything.

"Yeah, me neither. Unless it's simple."

"How's that?"

"Unless it's that I like having this TV broke." He laughed again. "Thing puts me right to sleep—working on it, I mean. I come in here, fuss with it for an hour or two, then I just stretch out on the floor here, right where I stand, and it's off to the land of nod."

I looked down at the floor, and sure enough there seemed to be a place the carpet had been tramped down some, pressed flat like grass will get when whitetail have been there. I nodded, half smiling along with him now.

"I get some trouble sleeping, too," I told him. "And the only thing for it is to work. It's been awhile since I've had any work to go to, though."

Which was the truth: I'd hardly slept a wink since Jake Lundeen asked me about that air compressor. When I did sleep, I dreamed I was awake, doing nothing.

Well the hotel clerk was giving me a funny look now, and I worried maybe did I say something wrong, did he see right clear through that cock-and-bull about the oil rig.

"That's right," he said. "That's about the only thing a body can do eight hours a day, that's to work. Can't drink eight hours a day. Can't eat eight hours a day. Work, that's about all a body can do to pass the time, and if a body works long enough, it goes to pieces."

He held his painted hand up, and for a moment or two we were quiet, thinking of the truth in what we'd said.

"I ask you something strange?" he wondered.

"Fine," I told him.

He reached into his pocket and fetch a pack of smokes, leaning against the doorframe.

"I've got the feeling you and me've met before," he said. "Just I can't think where or when."

And that smile in his eyes, it was just like Mike's. I'm telling you, they were each other's spit and image.

"Yeah," I said. "I know what you mean."

"I'm Carter," he said. "Carter Landreau. You need anything, it's me and Carlene up at the desk."

He smiled and put out his good hand, and I took it. A strong grip, and the skin of his palm thick and sturdy as old leather. "Pleased to meet you," I told him, and it was almost not a lie.

"Maybe it was on the rig," Carter Landreau went on, in a casual-type voice. "That's what I'm thinking."

"How's that?"

"I mean, maybe we met on the job. Claymore-Union, you said?"

"Yes," I told him, cause I was all in now, wasn't any taking it back. "Claymore-Union."

He watched me, nodding, tapping the smokes against the meat of his chest.

"Except they're Rubicon now," he said, smiling. "Claymore-Union been bought out. I know cause I used to work for Stafford."

And it was one whole day and one whole night before I knew what the hell Carter meant by that, not until I'd left Houston, when I was driving north quick as I could, and my eye catched on a great big billboard where that great big ugly city flattens out into sweet prairie and gray-green wood. Two boys in hard hats, smiling and shaking hands.

A BRIGHTER FUTURE TOGETHER, read that billboard. STAFFORD PETROLEUM IS NOW RUBICON OIL AND GAS.

And I felt like a right fool.

Maybe Carter Landreau hadn't guessed just exactly what I was up to in Texas, but he knew it didn't have much to do with roughnecking. He knew that, and still he never stuck his nose in any deeper. They're Rubicon now, Mr. Corliss: that's all he ever said about it.

"Well you look like you could use some shut-eye," he told me after a while. "And it's like I explained about the TV set. You let me know if you change your mind."

I told him I would, and then he cleared out. A decent fellow, that Carter Landreau. When I went out to fetch Clay's duffel bags, bring them inside, I thought to myself how we might've been friends, if the balls had broke a little different.

When I woke up that afternoon I didn't feel any less tired than when I'd put my head down. The sun had set outside, I could tell

31

even if the shades were drawed over the windows. By the bed, a clock read six minutes after five, and now I'd have to hurry some. I took out my wallet and found the piece of paper my brother give me the morning I left Colorado, the number I was supposed to call when I was ready to drop his dope off.

I punched zero for a local call and dialed it in, and now come a dry sort of voice I thought maybe I knew from someplace.

"Who the hell is this?" he asked.

"I need directions to the state fair," I told him, just like Clayton told me.

There was quiet now. That clock next the bed clicked over to seven minutes past five, and from outside I could hear the great heave and rumble of a diesel engine on the interstate, a semi going wherever it had to be. Then, real slow, this man told me how to get where I was supposed to be.

There were three of them waiting for me out back of this place, and they were big old boys, too, standing out on a cement platform next the freight door. When they saw me they commenced to pointing and waving their arms, like as if to shoo me away. I didn't know what it meant, and I got plenty nervous wondering. Like was it some kind of code or had something ugly happened, the Law or your drug bandit shootout, and I catched this weird vision and rode it out for a while: me taking off with Clay's dope and carrying it round with me forever, until my teeth fell out and I was old and gray.

But directly one of the three boys kind of jogged down the platform toward me, his hand making a gun pointed at the ground. So I pulled up and rolled down the window. It was a warm night, even a little bit hot, and my jacket hanging on me like lead now.

"We can't block the door," this boy called.

"Can't block the door?" I called back.

I waited. He watched me. Nothing happened. So I was like, "There's somebody else coming?"

But the boy never answered, and probably it was a stupid question.

I guess that place wasn't but two, three miles from downtown, and past the half-moon shape of the warehouse was the high-rise towers all lit up yellow and green. I watched them for a minute, wondering what to do. I thought about all them people who must live inside. In my mind they busied about like red ants. And for all that Houston felt like one great big empty room to me, and lonesome like all cities feel. And this was an evil place, this warehouse set in along other warehouses, the sort of place tricks you into believing all the world is as ugly as itself.

Meanwhile this big old boy sort of rubbing at the back of his neck, shy as a kid at the junior high dance. And I figured these boys must be about as nervy as I am, which made me feel a little better.

"I don't guess you're Abel," I said, when I'd got out my truck and come near enough I didn't need to shout.

"Abel's inside."

"Inside."

He nodded, pointing down the way he'd come. I looked over to where the rest of the crew were standing, just the other side of the platform. There was a great big bug lamp hanging over them, moths knocking against the bright.

Christmas Eve, this is, and I'm sweating like a pig.

I couldn't see a thing in that place, just cardboard boxes and the wobbly light from the bug lamp slanting underneath of the freight door. They had me set down the dope so as they could pat me down, thorough. One of these pretty boys, his arms so swole up with muscle they liked to tear right out the cotton of his tee shirt. He started up top, my back and chest and lift your arms, if you please, then down there, then down each side of my legs until he come to my jackboot and found Lij's Luger.

Don't bring no firearms, Clay had told me, and this pretty boy looked at it for a second, and then at each of his buddies, and then he made sure the breechblock was set and tucked it into the waistband of his jeans.

He said, "We'll just hold on to this until you get through with Abel."

So I told him, "Careful with that, that's an antique."

"I'll be careful, no problem."

End of this room was a steel door and through the door was pure dark, a room wide and high as a barn, and these two boys clicked on flashlights and we walked, three abreast and me in the middle, hauling the bags. I couldn't see anything but what stood ten feet at either side and in front of us, concrete floor and a wall of corrugated vinyl.

The sound your feet make in a room that big and empty.

So there we were, at what you call the moment of truth, and fear working on me like a poison. I remember my heart set to beating so hard that I felt it was liable to pop the buttons right off my shirt, and my body soaked through with sweat account of the warehouse was warm, and I hadn't took off my jacket, and the dope heavier and heavier the farther we walked into the darkness. Which is by way of telling you, I wasn't thinking straight. It wouldn't occur to me until later that if they'd wanted to take the dope without paying, they might've thumped me over the head the second I ducked under the freight door: all that worrying, Lord, all that worrying for two and a half grand. I still get a little razzed, thinking about it.

Well we must've walked clear crossed the warehouse before we come to this door, and through the door was a plain desk and nothing on the desk but a scale and a yellow legal pad and a pen, and setting behind the desk was this dude who couldn't be anybody but Abel.

And I stood there a while, not saying much of anything, and then Abel come out in that ashy voice I was sure I recognized now:

"So," he says, "you're Clayton's brother."

III

Clay never told us when he was coming, never give us any idea when to expect him. All the warning we'd ever get was the muffler on the Vette he got after he come back from the army, a jittery growl like some blood-hungry animal coming down Lij's lane. Lij was Momma's father, my granddad. It was his Luger that Abel's boys would take off me that night: Lij himself took it off a Nazi captain, in Cotentin. Anyway, him and me and May and Momma lived out at Lij's place, this was back in Crockett, Missouri. I guess this would've been a Saturday afternoon. If it was a Sunday then us four would've been in town, and if it was any other day besides then, me and May would've been in school. I wasn't fifteen that spring. That'd've made May seventeen, Clay I guess twenty-one.

You wouldn't think it to see him now, but Clay was a fine-looking man one point in time, the blast of that muffler like trumpets announcing some prince of olden days. I remember us waiting out on that porch when he come past the line of the woods, elbow out the window and his face shaved clean but his hair running down past his shoulders. And he pulled up out front with that easy smile on his face, the same one he'd had since he come back—discharged, Clay was, OTH—and he called up to Momma:

"Hey, you," he calls, "you're going to be a grandmother."

First I figured it was a joke. Clay was living in Texas them days, staying at his buddy's. We called my brother once a week, from the pay phone outside the Town and Country. This buddy of his—occurs to me now, I'm not sure Clay ever mentioned his name—had got Clay a job on an oil rig. Roughnecking, that's what he said he was doing down there. And all of us believed him cause back then there wasn't quite so many reasons not to.

Momma had worried herself gray when Clayton was over in Vietnam. Years after all this, after they'd locked my brother up, she worried herself dead. But that come later. Like I said, Clayton was working with this buddy of his down in Houston, and Momma got to speak to him once a week on the pay phone outside the Town and Country. I remember she used to dress up every time we called him, sort of make it an occasion. If it was winter Momma wore her brown dress and her hair down. In summertime, she wore her blue gingham dress and her hair done up in a braid.

She told Clayton the same thing every week before she give him the news: "We appreciate the help, Clayton," she'd say, "but are you sure you can spare so much?"

She meant the money he wired every month, the four hundred dollars we had waiting for us at the Western Union desk. I don't know how Clayton answered Momma, but she was the sort of person it was easy to lie to. Anyway, I don't like thinking about it.

After Momma it was May's turn to talk, and I remember how she used to razz our brother, how she used to wonder why he never asked for no raise so he could send more money home. May was just kidding him, of course. I guess she appreciated the money more than any of us: knew if it ever quit coming, she'd have to leave school and earn a wage. By the bye, that's exactly what happened. But I'm getting ahead again.

After May come Lij's turn on the phone. Lij would tell Clayton about the price of feed and antibiotics, about what pitiful little a bull was fetching at auction these days, about the bill from the veterinarian, and this was Lij's way of saying he didn't like taking Clayton's money but he didn't see any way around doing it. He was a tough old bird, I guess, to keep a loaded Luger under the driver's seat.

After Lij come my turn to talk. I asked Clay what it was like on that rig, what it was like to look round and see mile on mile of blue ocean. But my brother was always pretty short on details: "Pretty boring, Shell," he'd tell me. "What you want to know for?"

"Just curious," I'd answer, and it was almost the whole truth. Fifteen was young enough I still looked up to him and old enough I could hear the lie in his voice. I always let it go, let Clay tell about his favorite subject, which was females. And if you believed what he said then you'd think every girl in Texas was a six-foot Amazon in cowboy boots and all of them pretty much begging for poke. We must've spent two hundred dollars in quarters that year, but it didn't matter account of the money we had waiting for us every Sunday at the Western Union desk.

"We'd better get you down here, little brother," he used to tell me.

"Sure," I told him, "maybe your buddy can get me a job on that rig."

"Don't worry about that," Clay said. "Worry about getting you some."

So I guess you can see why I thought it must be a joke, Clay getting married. Her name was Nancy, he told us. She was a waitress

worked at a bar he went to sometimes. A waitress. And I can picture it perfect in my head like as if all this happened yesterday, Clay
setting at the red Formica table in the kitchen where Momma used
to read the letters he wrote her from Vietnam, the ones that turned
her hair gray. I can see him setting there, that same grin on his face:

"Well sure I'm going to marry her. It's the honorable thing, isn't it."

And it's like I told you, I looked up to my brother back then, but
that day there come this second voice buzzing in my ear: Honorable,
it said, what's he know about it? And hate will take hold of you like
sickness, and I felt it coming over me sure enough, this white-hot
fire behind my eyeballs, a fever. I tell you what, it made me afraid.

And the rest of them, May and Lij and Momma, smiling and
laughing to hear it, Momma even wiping the wet from her eyes
cause she was a very tenderhearted woman. I remember she asked
Clayton where him and Nancy was fixing to live, and Clayton said
they were going to save up for their own place but that for now
they'd just stay at his buddy's.

Lij nodded, sounded like a plan to him. He asked was the girl
from Texas and Clay said, no, she was from Great Spring, Arkansas,
that her daddy was still out there. And Lij nodded, said Great Spring
wasn't but half a day's drive from Crockett, and he asked what her
daddy did down there. And this whole while they're talking, I can
feel that same ugliness rising up and up inside of me. And when
Clayton answered him, "He's a minister. Church of the Pentecost,"
there come this feeling like somebody'd got hold of my tongue:

"Well that's pretty cute," I said. "Minister's kid in a shotgun
wedding."

And everybody gone real quiet, and my brother kind of looked
at me in such a way, like suddenly everything's going to be different. But it wasn't. He just tipped his head back:

"I guess my baby brother's grew up some since last I saw him," he laughed. "Shotgun wedding!"

Momma and Lij and May and me all laughed along with him, cause that was easier than the other thing.

When he visited, my brother never stayed more than a day or two before he headed south again. But the days seemed to move in slow motion, now there was this strange feeling between us two, and the air in every room like a string drawn taut. I heard him and Momma talking the morning he left. They must've thought I was asleep, but my room was right up next the kitchen and them walls thin as a matchbook.

"Shell's a chip off the old block, iddinee?" said Clayton.

And Momma going, "Hush, now, it's just growing pains. He's at that season of life."

And I remembered that voice that had come to me, struck out from nowhere, how I'd seemed to come upon hate coiled up like a snake in the dark.

And Clayton drives back to Houston and another month or two goes by, and summer comes on, the air thick enough to choke on it. And then once more I hear his Vette growling down the lane, and the four of us go out on the porch and sure enough here he is, and Mrs. Clayton Cooper setting in the passenger's seat. And when she steps out onto the lane she's wearing sandals like Jesus wears in an illustrated Bible, and a flowy white dress and sure enough her belly is flush up against the cotton: it's raised a good inch or two.

And they come up the steps and everybody shakes her hand, a little shy maybe cause Nancy was a real fine-looking woman back in them days, and when it come my turn I took her hand and looked into her antifreeze-blue eyes and down into her soul and I saw she was nothing but pure trash.

"Well you two look just alike," she said, shaking her head and laughing.

And that voice, I heard it again, hissing in my ear: I bet she opened her legs for every swinging dick in Texas before she met my brother.

And that was an unkind thought and maybe it wasn't even true. I fought it back, I stood there shaking her hand, and I believe I even managed to smile a little. Or I don't know, maybe I didn't have anybody fooled. I was the one who went to the Vette to fetch her bag out of the trunk, and I was the one who run it to the room where they would sleep, my room, even if thinking of them two in that bed about made me sick to my stomach.

I remember I stood there, listening to Nancy Cooper and Momma and May in the kitchen, chatting like they were best friends, their voices turning and keening like birdsong, that sharp shrill song of a woman well pleased with herself.

I dodged the kitchen, went round through the den and through the back door. And there was Lij and Clayton standing out on the back stoop. I knew well enough this was the place Lij liked to smoke, and I thought to myself I should've figured them two would be out here. I guess Mike Corliss was right when he said family's all you've got, which is by way of saying there's no running away from them, either.

"Where you going?" Clayton wanted to know. He smiled to say it, but just the same I didn't like him asking, didn't think it was any of his business.

"Nowhere," I said. "I was looking for y'all."

Us three stood there quiet for a moment, and I remember the wondering look in Lij's eyes, the way he watched me over the tip of that cigarette. It come to me, that same feeling as ever, like I'm the only one hasn't heard the joke, and I felt the fingers of my hands bunch into fists:

"What were y'all talking about?"

"I was just telling Clayton what Tom Meidecke said about May last week."

The Sunday past, after we'd got through talking to Clayton on the telephone, we'd run into the high school principal at the Town and Country. Mr. Meidecke told Momma and Lij that May was smart as a whip, that she was liable to end up a lawyer or judge. And now Clayton smiled in that way that made you love him, this sad and good-hearted smile:

"I believe he's right about that," he said, and the three of us stood there agreeing in the quiet, though a piece of me recollected that I had stood there with Lij and Momma that afternoon and Tom Meidecke hadn't said word one about me.

"Well what do you think?" Clayton asked me, giving a little nod inside toward the kitchen, where now Nancy's laugh blasted long and loud and clear.

"Think about what?"

"About what." He laughed. "About her."

And after a long quiet while, scrapping it out with that voice in my head, I told him what I really thought:

"Just wonderful, Clay," I said. "Some bitch to get a litter of pups by you."

And them two just watching me, their eyes hot as coals on my face, so hot I've got to look away: I'd never spoke like that, not in front of Lij I hadn't, and I wondered at that strangeness come over me again. And Clayton said he wanted to know just what in the fuck I meant by that, and Lij, who had went very pale in the face, said, "Easy, you two."

And I didn't have any kind of answer, either. I didn't know what I'd meant, what I'd said it for.

"I'm just kidding you," I told my brother. "I didn't mean anything by it."

And that was true, I guess, even if I heard that snake hissing in the back of my head: it cursed me for a hypocrite and a liar.

And Clay glared back, looking like he might still like to clobber me, but in the end he just said, "Well that's some joke." Meaning it was no kind of joke at all, and I ought not to've said it. And there was that feeling in the air again, of a string pulled taut.

I guess Nancy must've noticed I didn't talk much when she was around, that if she come in a room I found a reason to leave it. I guess she never needed anybody to tell her what I thought of her, and I guess what I thought never mattered much: she and May were like sisters before the sun had got round to setting, and Lij treating her like a second granddaughter. I believe Momma liked Nancy, too, although at supper that night she commenced to crying like she sometimes used to when she got her blues so bad, telling stories of Clayton when he was a boy, and of her own mother, who died when Momma was just a baby. Momma cried and cried, and that whole while Nancy holding to her hand and saying she understood just how Momma felt: Nancy had lost her own mother very young, too, from that same sickness Nancy has, the one that sets your muscles to jittering and jerking around. Which was apples and oranges, I figured. Nancy didn't know the first thing about it: the way our grandmother died was, she

emptied a can of kerosene over herself and went out into
and struck a match.

And I set there watching Nancy hold tight to Momma's hand,
and I couldn't help hating her a little, and I wonder sometimes did
Clayton see the look in my eyes. Did he hear that voice that was
me and wasn't, like the beginning of a storm in the dusky distance?

It was after supper, as Nancy and May begun to set in on a
great pile of dishes, my brother turned to me, nodding:

"Come on outside with me, bud."

Didn't anybody ask where we were going. I still wonder why.

We passed through the door and crossed the yard and went on
through the hitchgate and then down the lane and through the
woods. Lij had a pretty good-sized spread, I should mention,
about a hundred twenty acres, and we walked from one side clear
to the other—crossed the sinkhole, past the yellow glade where
water ran when we got rain and the heifers watching us with their
great big black eyes—and we didn't say one single word that whole
time. Then finally we come to this clearing in the woods, just the
other side of the cowpond. And that's when I saw them. His plants,
I mean. They stood up on a little ridge, a dozen or two dozen of
them, great big leafy fucking things, and a sump pump rigged to
pull right out of the cowpond to water them. For a while Clayton
was quiet, letting me take it in. Then he said:

"I guess you were bound to figure it out sooner or later."

I didn't say anything. I was too puzzled. Too something.

"You know what this is?" Clay wondered.

I didn't, but then all of a sudden I did: when Clay come up
from Houston, it wasn't just to visit. He was looking in on them
plants.

I don't know why I asked, "What about roughnecking? What about the oil rig?" By then I knew he'd never been on an oil rig, not one day in his whole life.

Clay shrugged: "That didn't work out."

"And that fellow you're staying with down there?"

"What about him?"

"He does the same thing, I guess."

"Probably the less you know about it, the better."

"And Lij?" I said. "Lij knows?"

I guess I asked account of feeling so young all of a sudden. So young, and so foolish. But Clay just laughed.

"Course," he said. "Who you think runs the pump when I'm gone?"

And we were quiet for a long while, and then Clayton told me what I still sometimes believe: "I do this cause I can't think of any other way."

And he carried on like that for a while, telling how nobody'd hire a man who was OTH, and so on, and then he turned to me and put his arms around me and said, "I love you, bud, I love you." And he wouldn't let me go until I'd said it back to him, which I did after a while, and back then it wasn't any lie. I mean, I did.

So Nancy whelped Erin in December '75, and before long she got pregnant again, and them three got their own place in Houston—not that we ever seen it, just we had a new telephone number to remember—and they traded in the Vette for something more practical, a dookie-brown Chevrolet Nova. Otherwise, things gone along like they had: Clayton come up once a month to visit and check up on his crop, except now he'd got Nancy and them wee babes a-suckling, and May started over at Southwest Missouri

State cause Tom Meidecke helped find her a scholarship there. And then one afternoon Lij and me and Momma drove into Crockett for the week's groceries and the money order and to call Clayton on the pay phone.

Except this week there wasn't any money order, and when we called my brother he didn't pick up the phone. Momma tried the new number once, twice, three times. And when she hung up for the third time she begun to cry a little. So me and Lij calmed her down, said not to worry, probably Clayton and his girls had went somewhere for the weekend and plum forgot to make the money order, we'd try again next week. But in my bones I knew the truth, I knew it meant trouble. The next week there wasn't any money order either, and nobody answered when Momma dialed the new phone number. After she'd hung up the pay phone, she begun to cry and to tell how she had a bad feeling.

"Something's the matter," she said. "He's disappeared. Vanished."

That was when I realized my brother had kept us separate, kind of fenced off from everything down there. We didn't have the foggiest idea what Clay got up to in Texas, apart from diddling a piece of Arkansas trash. All we had, it occurred to me, was a telephone number. And I thought of that evening when he bade me follow him outside. I thought about how I'd asked was his buddy in Texas helping with the dope, too, and what Clayton had said: the less you know, the better. Well now I knew.

When I told Momma to try the old number, she shook her head. She couldn't remember it. So this time I was the one who pumped one, two quarters in that slot and dialed the old number, the number of his buddy's place, and that phone rang and it rang, and I was just about to hang up when this voice struck out at me:

"What?" it said, not Hello?

I asked was Clay Cooper there.

"Who the fuck is this?" said the voice.

"This is Shelley. This is Clay Cooper's brother. Now tell me where he is."

"I don't know Clayton Cooper," the man said, and then he hung up the phone.

IV

I don't know much about the ugliness Clayton's got himself involved in. But one thing I'm sure of, it was this Abel's phone we'd been calling. It was Abel who told me he didn't know any Clayton Cooper. And standing there in that evil place, studying him, I recollected the two weeks we waited, wondering—two whole weeks—before that letter come in the mail marked GREAT SPRING, AR: Nancy Cooper, writing to tell us her husband had been arrested down in Texas on possession with intent to distribute.

It isn't often evil looks like itself, but this Abel fellow fit the bill pretty good: coffin-shaped face, eyes that same god-awful green of tornado sky. I thought he looked a little older than Clay, though it was hard to tell cause he had his head shaved down to the scalp. Seemed to look after himself, too, with this big swole of muscle where his shoulders and neck come together, and the veins in his arms trailing crossed twin tattoos of Jesus Christ crying.

"Yeah," I told him, "I'm Clay's brother."

And Abel said, "Well you look enough like him."

I set the bags down and nodded, watching him wait for me to say something.

When I didn't, Abel gone on: "He said you'd be quiet. I said, That's all right, I like quiet. Which as a matter of fact, I do."

He waited, watched.

"You know how long me and your brother go back?"

"Ten years," I said, cause it was '78 Clayton went down to Huntsville. But I guess Abel didn't get the joke. He just shook his head:

"Longer than that, baby brother."

And he pulled his shirt up past his arm to show me the tattoo he had on his shoulder, same one Clayton had got, the eagle head over the black shield and airborne over top of it all.

And I studied this fellow Abel, and I thought about what him and my brother must've saw over there together, and I thought about the hand-me-down jackboots I was wearing, and I wondered what it takes to turn a man wicked.

"Well." Abel took a deep breath. "Let's see how Clayton did."

Clayton, he called him. Like family.

He drew it out of the bags bit by bit with a metal spoon, and he set it on the scale, and then one of the boys I come in with put it all in a new bag, I couldn't say for sure why, and then he closed the new bag and bound it up with duct tape. Then they did it again, little by little by little, and Abel setting the figures down on the legal pad, taking his time about it, slow and exact as somebody marking the crown of a baseboard. Which I don't blame him for, either: I wouldn't have trusted my brother any much farther than I could shove him.

I was a little surprised when Abel tallied up the numbers and Clayton was right on the money: both them bags twenty-five pounds, one ounce. And there it was again, one and one: eleven, in other words.

When they'd added up all the figures, when my nerves had quit buzzing and I was just tired and bored out of my mind, it come time to take the money. Abel had it in a security box. The security box was just about the size of somebody's suitcase, but it didn't look like no suitcase account of it was stainless steel, with a stainless-steel hasp keeping it shut, and fit through this hasp a stainless-steel padlock.

A hot ache filled me up, now the last of my fear was gone.

Abel pushed the security box crossed the desk, and when I took hold of the padlock and asked just what the fuck is this, his eyebrows come about halfways up his forehead.

"That," he said, "is a padlock."

"I can see it's a padlock. How am I supposed to count it is what I'm asking you."

"Count it?" He looked confused, or just fake-confused. He said, "There's no counting, brother."

I told him no offense, it's just I'd like to see it's all there. And I think probably I was telling the truth. If I wasn't, I guess that means I was fixing to rob my brother from the get-go.

"This is what Clayton wanted," Abel said. Like a card dealer at the end of the night, he put his hands up and show his palms. He said, "This is what Clayton asked for."

"What do you mean it's what he asked for?"

"He asked me put this padlock on and send him the key."

"Send him the key?"

"That's what I said."

"And you already done it? You already sent the key?"

"I sent it three weeks ago, when he told me to do it."

Three weeks ago, he'd sent it, which was just exactly when I told Clay I'd run his dope for him. See what I mean?

"So he's got the key with him."

"Yes."

"So we won't count it until I get back to Colorado."

Abel didn't answer, just covered his mouth with his hand, and
that's when it struck me that Clay didn't want me to know how
much was in that suitcase. Meaning he didn't want me to know
just how much profit he was clearing. Why not? It's simple if you
know my brother like I do.

"How much is in there?" I asked. When Abel just blinked at me,
I asked him again. "How much? Ten thousand? Twenty?" And Clay
was fixing to pay me two and a half. And I guess I must've seemed
a little worked up, cause one of the boys I come in with said something quick and unfriendly in their lingo, and Abel held up his hand:

"Be cool, little brother. You got to relax."

I stared hard, daring him to give me more advice. Finally I
took up the security box and made for the door. I was thinking
to myself how it'd take me about two seconds, buddy, about two
seconds with a bolt cutters to work my way through that lock. But
by the time I made it back to my truck, I knew better. I wasn't going to use no bolt cutters, cause there was a red toolbox setting on
the floor of my room at the Seaside, and in the toolbox there was
Carter Landreau's hacksaw.

I got on the interstate and made my way back toward the hotel,
hunger whittling my mind down to a needle-sharp point. That city
spread crossed miles, great bands of ten-lane highway cutting over
of it like baling twine. I drove with the windows down, it was too
warm not to, and I took in the smell of the place, a smell like diesel and rot. After a while I pulled up to a McDonald's. Hamburger-
french-fries-and-Coke run me two and change. When I'd paid, I set
in the truck eating and watching the night. I didn't even know what I

was searching for until I looked crossed the street and saw the liquor store, the pay phone standing right out front of it.

I set in my truck a while, finishing my hamburger and watching the night fall apart. Palm trees and cracked pavement. You got the idea the world might like to swallow this city, the jungle might like to take back what's been stole from it.

That liquor store, a bright square against the night.

I drove crossed the intersection, turned off the engine. For a second I thought about bringing the security box in there with me, but then I considered how it would look. So before I walked over to the liquor store I set it behind my seat, and I covered up the metal real good with my jacket so none of it catched on the lamplight.

I got out, pushed through the door, nodded to the clerk.

"Make it quick, bud," he said. "We're closed in five."

"I'll make it quick," I said. The whole idea was: get some change, call my brother on the telephone, ask just what the hell gives, then crack the fucking thing and see how much does he have in there.

Liquor come in all kinds and colors, and all of it does pretty much the same thing. I passed the vodka and tequila. I passed the red and the white wine, the bourbon. Thinking to myself how of a sudden the world seems crazy and small. I found the Jack Daniels and hustled back to the register, I paid, I walked outside and felt that hot hunger. I thought about the road home, all shot to hell and the pavement split and ribbed, and I thought about the security box snug behind the seat, and Lij's Luger snug in the cuff of my boot again. In my hand, a bottle of Jack Daniels on sale for $11.99. What I'm saying, don't think for a second I was dumb enough to figure it would turn out all right.

It was exactly ten at night. I know cause the clerk from the liquor store was mean-mugging me while I dropped my quarters into the pay phone outside, drawing the grate crossed of the glass doors. I paid him no mind, just punched my brother's number in. Clay picked up after a long while, not sounding any too happy to hear from me.

"We'd better talk," I said.

"Talk about what?" he said.

"Talk about what. You know what."

"No I don't know. I honest to God don't know what you're calling me for when I've told you. Jesus, Shell."

"You know what I'm calling for."

"When I've told you not to call this phone while you're on this job. God almighty, Shelley, you don't listen, do you."

"I don't listen? Me?"

"I'm not going to talk to you. It's nine fucking o'clock on Christmas Eve."

"You and me are talking or so help me God I'll call you every hour on the hour till January."

"January?"

"Damn right, January."

"I'm going to see you in two days, when you give me what's mine."

"Yeah," I said. "About that."

He was quiet now, he knew I was serious.

"What the hell happened?"

"Nothing happened. I just have a few questions. About this padlock, for a start."

"About the padlock?"

We played telephone chicken for a while then, waiting to see who'd talk first. I won.

He said, "Well we can't talk just now."

And I said, "Why?"

And he said, "Cause my girls is still up."

"Fine," I told him. "I'll call you in an hour."

And when he didn't say anything, I told him, "One hour," and hung up the phone.

So I was still pretty razzed when I got back to the hotel room with the security box full of Clay's money, and the change I had from the liquor store about burning a hole in the pocket of my jeans. When I'd brought the security box and the road atlas and the whiskey inside, I set the box next the desk and set the atlas on top the bed and opened it up to T for "Texas." It was a two-page spread, account of this state's so goddamned big. I run my finger along the interstate blue. There was something steadying about doing it, like as if I'd already made it home, just by scooting my finger over the paper. And of a sudden I wanted to be back in Montgrand, back in Colorado and done with Clay's dope and Abel and this god-awful city. I wanted to be done with that money most of all, cause every time my eyes caught on that security box my blood was set to boiling again. I was digging in my pocket for my change, wondering if an hour had passed yet, when I heard a knock at the door.

And it was the devil himself standing there, smiling. "You got something to drink?" he wanted to know.

V

But before I explain about my dance with the devil, I guess I'd better tell you how her and me met. This was sometime earlier that day, after Carter Landreau had showed me to my room and I went to the parking lot to fetch them duffel bags out of my truck. That's when I saw her the first time. This long thin thing, all arms and legs, her bony chest kind of wedged between the door and the doorframe. She wore a white miniskirt didn't go halfway down her brown thighs, a black tank top didn't go halfway down her stomach. She might've been pretty, in a way she was a little pretty, but there was something about the bones in her face, that jaw like a thing you might cut your finger on, made her a little more than that. She had this thick streak of hair hanging over one shoulder and down practically to the small of her back, so dark it almost run to blue.

I see this girl, I can feel whole planets spinning in my guts. Whole constellations.

I guess what give her away was the voice, like a 45 record played at 33 rpm: how it sort of limped after me when she seen me crossing the parking lot: "Hey, you!" And the wobbly way she pressed against the door put me in mind of Momma toward the end, after they put Clayton away, strung so loose on them go-easy pills she could hardly see straight. A thought like that will chill you sure as a cold wind, and it chilled me to watch her there on that balcony, twisting like a tree afire.

"Hey, you!" she called out again.

And I knew there wasn't any good to come of answering her, so I didn't. I just brought them bags full of Clayton's dope on inside the room, shaking my head to show her what I thought.

"Hey, you," she called, again and again.

Finally, just outside the door, I turned to her. Called, "What?"

"You like to party?" she wanted to know.

"No," I told her, "I don't like to party." And then I turned the key and gone inside.

Which is by way of telling you, I know who's knocking before I turn the deadbolts and tug the door wide as the chain will let me. I stare at her through the crack and she smiles at me, not showing her teeth, the crooked sort of smile you give somebody when you like how they look. She doesn't seem half so stoned anymore, but her yellowy eyes have went a little sleepy, and the black part about as wide as a couple of manhole covers. She's slouching just like a kid will do, arms folded crossed her chest. And I try to think how old she is and I'm not sure, she might be seventeen or seventy, couldn't tell it for a fact.

She says, "You got something to drink?"

I don't smile at her to say it, but it's work not to: "You just cut right to the chase, don't you."

"You have?"

"No. I don't have."

"Yes you do. I seed you bring it in."

"Seen me bring what in?"

"I seen. I seen you bring the bottle in."

And if she seen me bring the bottle in, I'm figuring, then she seen me bring the money in, too. And you are wondering why I didn't close that door in her face right then. Truth is, I don't know myself. I was half-afraid of her, but then what does afraid have to do with some junkie turning the high beams on her smile? And she's just lonesome, I thought to myself, that might really be the issue here.

I said, "Forget it."

But just the same I couldn't help wondering what ruin had brought her here. A dangerous thing to wonder. You stare long and hard enough at a situation, it starts to seem like it isn't anybody's fault, just the chips have fell this way. Some minxy whore in the jungle night starts putting you in mind of the Holy Virgin, and vice versa.

Anyway, I half believed it by now, it's just she's lonesome, is what I thought to myself, she wants a drink on Christmas, that's all. But I knew it was a dangerous thing to be thinking when you've got a security box full up of somebody else's money.

"No drink," I told her, when I'd got my mind right again.

And she said, "Later, I'll come back later."

And I said, "Tell you what. Come back tomorrow."

And she said, "Tomorrow I will leave."

And I said, "Yeah. Me, too. That's why I want you to come back then."

And she just stared at me all sleepy-mad as I swung the door shut in her face.

And when she was gone that security box give me a queer feeling, like as if the whole night was watching me and just as hungry as a tiger. I wanted to be quit of that money, and I figured the sooner I was, the better. You try walking around with a suitcase like that sometime, it isn't as easy as it sounds.

When I'd checked the blinds were shut, I walked back to the bed and run my finger along I-10, the highway that cuts west crossed all of Texas. When my finger hit El Paso, I flipped to N for "New Mexico," and I found I-25, which run from the border clear up through Albuquerque and on into Colorado. All the way to Wyoming. I thought about home and I thought about how much was in that security box and I wondered how much was enough to kill somebody over. Twenty grand? Thirty? And what would Clay do if I took a quarter of that? A half? The only way I know how to explain it: I couldn't not know how much was inside.

So I walked over and fetch Carter's hacksaw out of the toolbox. Got to work.

The padlock fit that hasp so tight that the brass housing was shanked up at an angle and I couldn't hardly get at the loop. I had to half set there, one foot up on the mattress and the other one planted on the floor for leverage: sucking back air, working away at that steel for so long that the metal grew hot to the touch and the juice went out of my arm. Guess I would've made quite a sight, but nobody could see me through them blinds.

When I stopped after maybe a quarter hour, I hadn't took but the tiniest little fleabite out of the padlock, never mind I'd yanked just about all the teeth from Carter Landreau's hacksaw. I'd gummed it up, far as I could tell, and I don't just mean the saw. I mean trying to crack the damn thing in the first place. Shame on me is the shape of what I was thinking to myself when I pulled the coins out of my pocket: a quarter, three dimes, two pennies. This was enough change yet to call Clayton, but I didn't go for the door right away. Instead I just set there a minute, looking at the coins in my hand, the silver next to the copper.

Shelley, I thought to myself, you are a fool.

And so I fetched up the hacksaw again, and this time I went at the brass. The housing, I mean. And you can't cut through steel with a hacksaw but brass isn't no trouble at all. And I'll tell you, I don't guess it took me but half a minute, Carter's hacksaw just peeling through the metal. I cut through the front, then each side, and when I'd hacksawed clear through to the shackle I went to get the plumber's mallet from out of Carter's toolbox and bust it loose. I figured I could just bend the shackle out of the lock, which I was right about that.

And I was just about to open up that case and see what's inside when that little bitch knocked at the door again.

I still can't tell you why I answered her. Not twice, but three times. Still I knew there wasn't any good could come of it. But then I've got the chain fit crossed the door, never mind the Luger in the cuff of my boot, and apart from that that she was scrawny to do me much harm, and high as a kite besides.

That same crooked grin, the cracked and chewed-at lips making the words: "Look, one drink we have."

"We what?" I said, glaring at her through the slit in the door.

"I have," she said. "You have. I go away."

"You want to try that one again?"

"Drink," she said.

"I thought you said you were coming back tomorrow."

"I can't come tomorrow."

I'm telling you, this girl could make whole speeches with a smile. And now she give me the sort that'll get ideas across it wouldn't be right to put into words, all gums and cracked teeth.

And I told her, "If you think I'm letting you in this room, you're out of your goddamn mind."

"It won't take long," she promised, kind of tipping herself onto the balls of her feet.

"It won't take any time at all, sweetheart," I told her, "cause I ain't letting you in this door."

And her voice come like somebody talking in his sleep: "You're mean. You're nasty."

And this gal standing there when I shut the door in her face, her grin in the middle of a sentence that fills me with a warm itch. And now I fetched the plumber's mallet out of Carter's toolbox, and knocked the shackle clear of the housing. Opened it wide.

It looks about like it does in the pictures: them fifty-dollar bills stacked neat as two-bys at a lumberyard, and each of them bound with a strip of brown paper that reads $5,000. They fit pretty snug in there, five in one row and five in the next. Five plus five is ten, ten times five thousand is fifty thousand. And twenty-five hundred, in case you don't feel like doing the math, is a five percent cut.

You want to know what fifty thousand dollars cash feels like? It feels like a blind rage. Like a wolf howling at the moon. I thought of my brother playing Santa Claus. Handouts for Mike and May and little Layla, and this job he's gave me like it's some kind of favor.

All that was nothing, I realized. Just crumbs off his plate.

I set there looking at this money while the night seemed to scream out at me. And my hands making fists and my jaw biting down hard on nothing. And I know of some who would've said half to grow it and half to run it. I know of some who would've took more, I know of some who would've skivved all that money and lit out. But then you can't do that to your own brother, can

you. One, two, three stacks: that's all I took. To this day I'm not exactly sure why I took fifteen, but it works out to about three grand
for every year he did in Huntsville.

My plan, if you want to call it that, was to get a new padlock on
my way back to Colorado. Clay wouldn't know the difference until
after I'd dropped the money off and his key didn't work. But when
I picked up the security box to set it underneath of the bed, I heard
the stacks clunking and jumping around inside, somehow it made
you nervous. So I looked around for something to keep the rest
of the stacks flush. The phone book they kept on the bottom shelf
of the nightstand was a little too wide and the weight felt wrong,
besides. I tried one of the towels in the bathroom after that, but I
couldn't get it clear of the hinges. After the towel I walked back to
the nightstand drawer and found a King James Bible, and I'll be
goddamned if it wasn't about a perfect fit.

Under the bed it went.

There was a pay phone outside the manager's office, but before I
went out there I looked around for some place to put my cut. Fifteen
grand: you don't like to leave so much money out in the open air.
And don't ask me why I didn't just set it in the toolbox. Don't ask
me why I didn't just set it in the drawer of the nightstand, where the
Bible had been. Don't ask me why I didn't just set it in the dresser,
the pillowcase, the medicine cabinet, behind the toilet. Don't ask me
what witchcraft made my eye to catch upon the television set.

I lay the stacks in, one up top and one each on the sides. Then
I stuffed the red- and yellow- and blue-wire guts back in, and I set
the panel over top of it all. After that, I found the Phillips head
in Carter's toolbox and screwed the panel in place again. Now it
looked about like any TV set you ever saw, but still I stood there a
while studying it, scared to go but feeling a little too mean not to.

My brother answered the phone in a tight whisper, but I let my voice carry high and far crossed that parking lot. I told him in a half shout, "A padlock."

His answer wasn't any kind of answer at all: "Careful what you say on this phone."

"Won't be me doing the talking," I said, hoping he could hear the smile in my voice. "All I want's an explanation."

"About what?"

"What you did it for."

"What'd I do what for?"

"What do you think? What'd you set a padlock on the security box for?"

"That's it?" he said, sounding like he didn't quite trust what he was hearing. "That's what you're so razzed about?"

When I didn't answer him, he went on: "What do you think there's a padlock on there for? So none of it goes missing."

Which, maybe that made sense. Some of it already had went missing. But then I knew it must be more than that.

"Want to know what I think?" I asked him, knowing he didn't. "I think you didn't want me to know what kind of profit you were clearing."

"You think wrong. Besides, wasn't my idea."

My brother, he's a shifty SOB. My words dried up then, wilted, went dusty in my throat. After a while I told him, Bullshit. I told him what Abel told me, about sending the key in the mail and so on. And Clay said, sure, all that was true, but just the same the padlock wasn't his idea.

And I said, "Whose idea was it then? Nancy's?"

And Clay said, "Never you mind whose idea, little brother, there's no changing it now."

I stood there, quiet. It felt like Clay was trying to hamstring me, but I couldn't see the long game yet.

"Well if it's like you say, then how come you still haven't told me how much is inside that box?"

"You really want to know?"

"Yes."

"You really, really want to know?"

"Yeah, you bastard. I want to know."

"Twenty thousand," he said. "That's how much."

"Twenty thousand."

"That's what I said."

"You're a lying bastard," I informed my brother, after which it was his turn to set quiet on the other end of the line. I could hear him wondering, putting it together now, thinking to himself I might just be crazy enough to try cracking the steel.

"Twenty thousand," he said, and his voice was afraid, "and it better all be there when I see you day after tomorrow."

"Better all be there, or what?" is what I wanted to know. But the line'd went dead.

What I thought about, heading back toward room fourteen: twenty thousand is just exactly right. That number was big enough to believe, maybe it was even big enough to get a little sore over. But it wasn't necessarily big enough I'd ask him for a bigger cut. Twenty-five hundred was better than ten percent of twenty grand, after all. Not so bad.

I thought, too, about how Clayton had said it: Twenty thousand, bold, without so much as a hitch in his voice, without your moment's hesitation. So maybe you can understand why I begun to change my mind about how much I was fixing to take, why even fifteen thousand didn't seem like enough, all the sudden. Maybe you can understand why I figured I'd better take thirty instead. I saw myself handing him the security box with the busted padlock and twenty thousand dollars inside. Twenty grand, I'd tell him, just like you said. And I saw Clayton's face when he knew I'd got the better of him.

I was thinking to myself that it was a fine night, that I liked the warm clean feel of the air on my skin. I believe I must've still been smiling like a madman or an idiot when I come up to my room and saw Carter Landreau standing outside, tapping at the door, going:

"Mr. Corliss? Mr. Corliss, sir?"

Carter has a hand truck with him, and at his feet is a great big cardboard package and crossed the package is the word MAGNAVOX. And Carter Landreau is tapping at the door, calling out in a soft voice, "Mr. Corliss, sir? Mr. Corliss?" And I think to turn and walk off back the way I come, but I've left the light on in the room and he might suspicion something, and anyway he's heard me by now, he turns to me, smiling, going like:

"Merry Christmas, pal."

And I don't know how to answer him, so I don't, I just stand there with the key to room fourteen in my hand and ice water pumping into my veins. And Carter just a-smiling the whole time, cause he doesn't know he's fixing to steal fifteen large from me.

"Mr. Landreau, you've surprised me," I think to tell him.

The mannequin hand is gone, now Carter wears a mean-looking hook. And with his hook he reaches round the middle of the hand truck and tip it back. He nods at me, I guess waiting for me to make a move to unlock the door. Which, you probably figured, I am not about to do anytime soon.

"This a bad time, Mr. Corliss?" he asks after a while.

"Being honest," I tell him, "a little."

He is still smiling, but I know it's more than just friendliness makes him say, "It won't take me but five minutes, I've just got to—"

But I don't let him finish.

"Like I told you," I say, "I don't mind about the TV. I don't watch much TV. I'm in here reading my Bible."

And it hurts a little, that look Carter gives me.

"Which book, Mr. Corliss?"

And him calling me Corliss when I feel like I'm standing here, looking at the dude. Honest, them two could've been brothers. And like some cheapy copy of the real deal, all I can think to do is say his words back at him, an echo moving crossed a great quiet.

"Which book?" I say.

"Which book of the Bible?" he says. "You said you were in here reading your Bible, I'm asking you which book."

And a thought runs through me I won't know how to put words to, not for hours. Not until it's too late. The man's testing me, I can see it in them blue-as-a-jay eyes. And when I answer him— say, "I'm reading the Book of Luke, Mr. Landreau"—he looks at me like he knows better. Like he knows everything.

"Mr. Corliss," he says, "now I want you to understand this. There's no guests allowed."

"I don't have no guest in there. I swear it."

I can tell he wants to believe me, which is almost the same as believing. But his look is puzzled, probably he can't figure out why I haven't opened the door. Why I'm just standing here.

"Pretty tuckered," I tell him. "Otherwise I'd offer you in for a drink."

"Teetotal." He shrugs, and I might've figured. His eyes aren't half as suspicious anymore, maybe he even believes what I've told him about me and the Book of Luke. But he isn't done asking questions yet:

"Your meeting went all right, Mr. Corliss?" And when I just stare at him, he says, "The meeting you had this evening?"

"Yes," I say, "it went fine. It went all right."

He kind of shakes his head, thinking his thoughts aloud: "Well Carlene's not going to know what to make of this. She told me, stop this craziness of fixing that busted television set. You run out and get that boy in fourteen a new TV for his room."

Still I have nothing worth saying. And so we stand there a little while, each of us waiting for the other fellow to talk, and then finally Carter Landreau says:

"You're just plain not going to open this door, Mr. Corliss, are you?"

And what answer is there to make? What answer worth making, I mean.

Now he sets the television down and reaches in the pocket of his red sweater and come out with a little bit of something bound up in a paper towel. He watches me unwrap it, careful and slow, and inside it is a sugar cookie shaped like a fucking Christmas tree.

I tell you, I've never felt so lonesome in my whole life.

You want to know how lonesome and rotten I was feeling? When that girl asked my name, I told her. My real name, too, not some phony one like Bob Jones or Jim Smith. The whore had kept her word, anyway: said she'd come back tomorrow, and sure enough it was quarter after midnight on December 25, 1987, when she knocked at the door. Christmas, I mean.

I answered same as I had, "Hell do you want?" But I reckon she knew I was glad to see her. And that's the funny thing about all this business, I think I must've half wanted it to go south. I smiled to watch her blow inside—this time I hadn't bothered fastening the chain—smiled even if there was a sweet sad voice in my head, ringing like a church bell: You will regret this, it went, you will regret this, you will regret this. Momma's voice, I think it must've been.

But still I set there, smiling, even a little relieved. Lying to Carter Landreau had gave me a lonesome and low-down feeling. I was in that great big god-awful city, it seemed to me, without one single friend. Never mind the padlock I'd cracked out of pure cussedness, or the money Clayton had knew better than to trust me with.

"Shelley?" she said, while I poured a good-sized slug into one of the Styrofoam cups they kept by the sink in the bathroom. "That's a woman's name."

I brought the Jack and Coke out to her on the bed, where she was setting, kind of leaning back on her hands with her legs crossed. She looked good.

"Sure," I said. "Sometimes it's a woman's name. But sometimes it's just short for Sheldon. That's me."

"Sheldon," she said. "I like this better."

She had an accent thick as salted butter, though I never got around to asking where she come from, or how she'd ended up in a steaming pile of shit like Houston. And even if I had asked, I don't believe I'd have got a straight answer. She said her name was Candy, Candy for Candace. And the way she said it give me the feeling she'd heard it in a movie or a TV show. So I said, "You're full of shit."

She said, "I'm shit?"

"Full of it," I said. "You lie. Candy's an American name."

And she said, "I'm American."

And I said, "The hell you are."

69

And this time she didn't answer me, just half closed those yellowy eyes and looked round the room like she couldn't believe a place could be so boring. My God, you never saw somebody so sore. After a while I said I was just messing her, I didn't mean anything by it. And that's when it happened, something I still don't have the words for. She seemed to change her mind about me, or maybe I mean she seemed to make her mind up. She patted the space next hers on the bed.

What was it kept me standing there, watching the shadows do wicked things to her face? That exact same feeling of walking into a room and realizing you're the one everybody's been grousing about, that's why it's got so damn quiet all the sudden. What I'm telling you is: I knew the truth. In my heart, anyway, I knew it. She'd saw me bring that security box in the room just like she'd saw me bring that bottle of liquor, and the only reason she's setting here is she thinks she might get to see what's inside.

But I am getting ahead of myself. Cause it wasn't ever as simple as some whore cracking me over the head with a bottle of whiskey and taking Clayton's money. I believe I was under some kind of spell. Or maybe I just mean, she had a way of tricking you into saying more than you meant to. Like when she wondered where I come from, and I told her Montgrand, Colorado, and she set there smiling at me a minute:

"Liar," she said.

And I explained how, yeah, it was a sort of lie, account of my people were from Missouri, but that we come out to Colorado after the government took the spread, civil forfeiture, which she didn't know what that meant. And I explained how it just meant the government taking your land cause you're doing something with the land you oughtn't, and she wanted to know doing what, exactly, and I had to tell the whole boohoo story. How Clayton had been growing dope out there, but that it was Lij they busted account of the land was in his name, and so forth. I talked like a thirsty man drinks. And in the back of my mind is this voice telling me shut up, be quiet, get her out of this room.

She just listened. She listened, smoking them Marlboros one after the other. Soon as she poked one out in the ashtray, she'd be fiddling with the book of matches she had tucked in the cellophane. By the time one in the morning come round, I believe she'd had about half a pack.

"Smoking'll kill you," I said. "Sure as a bullet, it will."

She just set there, blowing smoke rings into the quiet. "Of course," she said, "sure as a bullet." And a shiver gone down my spine.

"What do you do for a job?" she wanted to know after a while.

And I told her, "Guess."

"I guess you're a police," she said.

"No." I laughed.

"No?"

"No. I'm a carpenter."

"You're a liar."

"No. I'm telling you true. I frame houses."

And she watched me for a second, making her mind up not to believe me. Said, "You're a police. I know."

I promised her again I wasn't. I went out first thing every morning, I said, built sunup to sundown. Framing house, working eight hours a day.

She said, "Promise me."

"Yes, I promise. It's all true."

"No," she said, "promise me you're not a police."

And suddenly it hit me, what she'd asked for. Suddenly everything was simple again. Suddenly I was just some john in a hotel
room with his date.

"Scout's honor," I told her, and she laid her lips on mine.

There isn't anything in this world more god-awful than a man
who likes to brag about who and what all he's screwed. This fellow
Wicklowe I used to know, this was back in Missouri. Wicklowe'd
set at a stool in the Go-Go Room for an hour or three, talking
about some piece of ass he'd had when he was younger, some girl
in Texas or North Carolina or Arkansas . . .

. . . could fit her legs all the way behind her head, boy . . .

. . . screamed bloody murder when you give it to her, boy . . .

. . . wasn't but sixteen year old, boy . . .

And this whole time you can't quite forget it's Jarvis Wicklowe
telling you this story, Jarvis, with his smile like a rusty razor, and
it's his skinny white ass you've got to picture pumping like a piston.
Paint dried quicker.

So I'm not going to set here and tell you every itty-bitty detail,
but let me just explain that this girl Candy knew what she was
doing. I mean to tell you, she was a professional. We necked on the
bed for a while, and then she begun to run her hand up and down
my leg. Up and down, down and up. Then she commenced to give
me a little squeeze, so that I liked to've popped like a teenager at a
drive-in movie.

"Twenty dollars," Satan said after a while. She had undid the
top button of my pants and got it loose from the fly and out in the
open air. Said it again: "Twenty dollars."

And I shook my head. I said, "No. No dollars."

And she said, "Fifteen."

Her hand was cold, but it felt all right just the same, and she set there working me like that, looking up at me like she was waiting for something. And I suppose I must've been in a strange frame of mind, cause for the life of me I couldn't think what.

"Just mouth," she said after a while. "Ten dollars."

"Fine," I said.

Now she got down on her knees in the space between the beds and did it for a while with her mouth.

And everything was going about like how you'd figure: it's your ordinary everyday business-type interaction between a lady of the evening and her john. But right when I'm about to pop, that feeling come back to me, that feeling like walking into a room and it goes all quiet. I felt myself to sink through the very bed, I felt myself sinking deeper and deeper, though the floorboards, through the concrete and clay, through sand and bedrock, down into the bowels of the earth. And I saw something down there, jet-black and flowing like water, smooth-turning like a snake's skin.

And that is hell. I went to hell, and hell looks like nothing at all.

When I opened my eyes, the whore was smiling at me, mouth closed tight around the gunk and one hand held under her chin. But the light in here was too strong, it was doing some mighty unkind things to her face: digging trenches at each side of her mouth, spreading blue-black shadows where they oughtn't to've been. I didn't like what I saw, and it must've showed in my face cause she stood and walked quick over to the bathroom. I watched the doorway, nervous about a thing I couldn't name yet, listening to the water running in the basin.

She called out to me, "It feels good?"

I didn't answer. My head was heavy, and I commenced to digging in my pockets for what I owed. We'd settled on ten, but all I had on me was pennies and one solitary twenty-dollar bill.

I leaned forward and catched her eye in the mirror over the washbasin, and that's when I knew I wasn't going to pay, not one red penny. She lifted the bottle to her lips and swished the booze around in her mouth for a second before spitting it out.

"That ain't mouthwash" was all I could think to say.

Well she just looked at me, I guess not much liking what she saw. And of a sudden I was awake out of this dream the devil'd put me in, and I could see him clearly now: this long thin boy with an almost pretty face, the devil himself standing here in this room and I am afraid.

"Who in hell are you?" I said.

But he didn't answer, not exactly. He just come and stand over me: "You pay now," he said.

I set my face in my hands. I didn't look up, not even when I said, "Get your ass out of here."

He just stood there, like, "Give, pay. Give, pay."

And then I heard the devil walking over to the bathroom sink, not in any rush about it, and fetch that bottle. What I told you earlier? How I must've half wanted it to happen? Half wanted to lose that money? What I was thinking, the second or two before he cracked me over the head with that whiskey bottle: What are you waiting for, girlie? Go on ahead and do it. So that's pretty much how I ended up in Kansas City, calling my ex on the pay phone from the bus station.

VI

Truth is, Syrena and me was Mike's fault: he's the one to blame. He's who turned to me that too-hot afternoon beginning of September. The four of us ought to go out sometime, he said. Double dutch, I mean. And I remember him smiling at me while my guts turned somersaults.

Mike Corliss was different back in them days, full of piss and vinegar. He had a smart mouth on him, and he wasn't afraid to use it, either, which is why Laughton Starbuck kind of had it out for him.

"Where's your protective eyewear, Corliss?"

"My protective eyewear?"

"That's what I asked you."

"My protective eyewear's protecting the dashboard of Sheldon Cooper's truck. That's where I left it this morning."

Sheldon, he used to call me, cause he knew it got on my nerves. To anybody else I was Shelley.

I was just a journeyman back then. I drove Lij's truck to work and home every day, give my best friend Mike Corliss a ride. Half the time, he'd forget something on the dash: that blue bandana, that pack of smokes, that pair of goggles.

I guess I looked up to Mike, who was a couple years older than me and besides that had what you might call a way about him. He told a story better than anybody I knew, for one thing, though you never knew how much was true and how much he'd half made up. He told me how a honeybee flies through the rain, missing every drop. He told me nobody'd ever saw a giant squid, but even so scientists know they exist cause sometimes, he said, a whale or a shark will wash up on the beach, a great big bite took out of it. He told me *Close Encounters of the Third Kind* was a true story, he knew somebody who knew somebody thought he had aliens playing music in his head, then about ten years ago, poof, this dude just vanished.

You knew better than to believe everything he said, but then if you ever doubted his word Mike'd just get real quiet.

"Fine," he'd tell you. "Believe me or don't. I don't care." And kind of sulk after that. Cause Mike had a temper on him, too, maybe he still does.

And the stunts he used to pull. Take for example what happened with that bowling ball he'd stole from the alley in Birch Tree. For a couple weeks we'd kept that thing, a thirteen-pounder, in the back of Lij's truck, set inside a spare to keep it from punching a hole in the bed. One evening we come up on the Go-Go Room, and Mike calls out to me: "Stop the car, damn it! Stop!" So I pull into the lot.

When I turn to him, Mike's pointing to this beautiful baby-blue Chevrolet C30 with a custom decal on one door: STARBUCK AND PURCHISS CONSTRUCTION LLC, it reads.

Mike is saying, "Go a little closer, Sheldon."

So I do. I pull closer, even though I already know what he's fixing to do, even though I don't like it. "Don't," I tell him, but my breath catches and anyway he's already out the truck and reaching into the spare for that bowling ball and heaving it through Laughton Starbuck's windshield. The whole thing come out at once. A kind of glassy scream. And I am afraid, cause I know I can't afford to lose this job, and cause Mike is taking his time coming back to the truck. He pulls the blue bandana out his back pocket and kind of dabs at his forehead. Takes that pack of smokes out his shirt and lights up.

He takes a big drag, gets in.

"Well," he says, "what are we doing now?"

You got the feeling around Mike that he was liable to go too far one day. You got the feeling he was liable to go too far, and you'd let him.

We framed house for three years together before he left. I guess you might be wondering how a boy like that held on to a job for so long, and truth to tell it had always stumped me. There were plenty on that crew who would've liked to see Mike go, by the way, in fact me and Lij were about the only people in Austin County who seemed to think much of him. Not even my sister liked him, not back then she didn't. Mike come over to supper once or twice a week. He set there telling jokes until my ribs were sore and my grandfather was pounding on his chest, trying to get his wind back: "You hear about that swamp rabbit, Lij?" But all that while, May was quiet, the look on her face like she can't reach an itch. She'd been touchy since they locked Clayton up in Huntsville and she had to quit school, and Momma passing hadn't improved things much, neither.

"I can't stand him, Shelley," May told me one morning, this would've been the spring after Momma died. "He's just so goddamned arrogant."

I never took it all that serious. Most people didn't know Mike Corliss had a quiet side to him, too, that you could talk to him about things you couldn't talk about with other people. I told him about Momma's accident, how I was the one who found her that day, her face blue as jeans. I fessed to Mike what I'd never fessed to anybody, not even myself. That Momma dying was Clay's fault, account of she'd been out of her mind with grief since the day they locked him up. Mike would listen, something like a smile on his face:

"Well look, Sheldon," he told me once. "I don't see how that's his doing. I mean, ain't like he made her take 'em."

The go-easy pills, he meant. And I guess I sulked a little, not answering, knowing he was wrong but just the same hating the sense in what he said. And he reached out and took hold of me, his hand very warm on my shoulder, breath a kind of buzz on the back of my neck:

"Look, bud," he said. "Forget it. I'm sorry."

What all I'm about to tell you happened back in '80, which was one whole year after Jimmy Carter gone fishing in Georgia and a rabbit swum up to his boat and bit him. That was the joke back then, the one we'd been telling for a year and still hadn't got old. Like that afternoon, after Starbuck shut off the generator, and me and Mike made our way over to the truck and get in.

"You seen any swamp rabbits today?" Mike said.

"Swamp rabbits? No more'n usual."

"Haven't had to fight any off, I hope?"

"Just a few. The swamp rabbit is docile this time of year. The heat gentles him."

"Gentles him?"

"Chills him right out, Mike."

"But he remains a dangerous beast."

"Dangerous as they get, Mike."

We were quiet after that, the miles ticking along. And then Mike said, "I hope Ray don't mind buttered toast for supper, cause butter and bread's all we got at the house just now."

Ray was Ray Corliss, Mike's dad. Forgot to mention, this was a couple years after Ray got bad sick and Mike's momma cut and run. Before that, you heard stories about them two. Black eyes, cracked ribs, busted teeth. Most people hadn't blamed Rose Corliss when she left like she did, though I wondered what Mike thought of all that. And the thought occurred to me sometimes, Mike's secrets were tall tales, by and large. But then I knew him well enough where it mattered. About his dad's supper, for example, Mike meant he wanted to come eat with us, and he wanted May to fix him a plate to bring home.

"Come over our place," I told him. "We got plenty."

And Mike said, "Well I don't know."

"Sure," I told him. "Won't take long, have you home before the swamp rabbits are up and about." Meaning, by dark or so.

And we'd had this same conversation a hundred times, and a hundred times Mike had come over and put me and Lij in a fit while May set there grinding her teeth, watching Mike eat the food he never bothered to thank her for. Except that afternoon, May had company of her own.

I hardly noticed her, even though I decided later on she was the kind of girl you notice: full-figured. I know May must've introduced us. I know I must've learned Syrena's name. I know I must've shook Syrena's hand. I know she must've explained, or maybe May did, that they worked together at the J.C. Penney's in West Plains, in the home appliance section. Problem is, I don't really remember all that. It was about like any other supper—couldn't even tell you what we ate—except there were five of us at the table instead of the usual three.

When we finished, me and Mike got in the truck. I'd been true to my word: it was well before sundown. He shut the door after him, that plate covered in tinfoil settled into his lap, his daddy's supper.

"She had eyes for you, Sheldon," Mike said.

And I said, "Who?"

And he said, "Who you think?"

So I thought. After a beat, I said, "Syrena?"

"Yes, shit-for-brains."

And I told him all the things you're supposed to when you hear something like that: "Naw" and "You're full of it" and "She wasn't ever." But I couldn't help smiling a little to say it. And by the time I pulled onto the highway, Mike Corliss was working around to his big idea: "We ought to go out sometime, the four of us. Double dutch, I mean."

And I was quiet, trying to decide if he was serious. And then Mike said: "Missed the turn, shit-for-brains."

That summer, we were working on this cabin. Now we aren't talking Abe Lincoln out there with his axe and a pail of tree sap set to boil over a fire. No, them log cabins come in a kit, with the grooves already cut in the joists, and the splines and eleven-inch screws in a shrink-wrapped crate. I swear it to you, that first pack of lumber come with a set of directions.

We were pretty much through with the frame by now. And it was big, too: two floors, six bedrooms, three and a half bathrooms. There were two chimneys, two fireplaces, one on each side. Dude owned it was a lawyer from Chicago, he was only fixing to live there for a few weeks out of the year. Even so, he wanted a custom finish on the beams, hardwood flooring, and cedar cabinets. About the only thing made it a cabin was the lumber in the frame.

And when the drywall crew come and piled that Sheetrock alongside the place the front door was supposed to go in—dude wanted glass doors, I forgot to tell you—I pictured them laying that plaster over top of that beautiful white pine and felt sick to my stomach. We were working on the deck that day, since the drywall crew was busy inside. All that morning and into the afternoon, me and Mike Corliss and Jarvis Wicklowe were out front of the lot with a couple spud bars and a posthole digger, trying to find the freeze line.

That's hard work, by the way. Spend a couple hours digging postholes, your shoulders are liable to feel like they might slide right out the sockets, and the muscles in your back clench up just like a fist. It isn't work to talk through, but Jarvis Wicklowe just talked and talked, telling about some piece of ass he'd had in Arkansas, and it was like somebody drilling screws in your ears, and that sun that seemed too hot and close for September wheeled into the sky. And then finally Mike Corliss told him, "Jesus's sake, Wicklowe, shut your damn mouth," and Wicklowe went quiet, and then Mike turned to me:

"Well, Sheldon," he said, "how about it?"

"How about what?"

"How about my chances?"

"Chances of what?"

"Marrying May."

While that dumb son of a bitch Wicklowe sniggered, I fiddled with the grip of the digger, trying to make the whole world vanish.

"Honestly, bud," I told him after a while, "I don't think you got much of a chance at all."

Mike laughed, so did Wicklowe, but I could tell he didn't much like hearing it. It was nearly quitting time by then. The quiet had hardly settled in again when Laughton Starbuck pulled up in that baby-blue Chevrolet C30 with the words STARBUCK AND PUR-CHISS CONSTRUCTION LLC on the side, the brand-new windshield. He razzed us some, saying how we hadn't dug but half of the postholes we needed for this deck.

Well me and Wicklowe were quiet, kicking the dust at our feet. But Mike went: "We can stay longer, you want. But I'm taking time and a half."

And Starbuck give him a look, and Mike took that blue bandana from the pocket of his jeans and pushed the sweat off his forehead. Our whole lives we'd been waiting for something to happen, but it never did. And now Starbuck just spit in the dirt and went on over to check on the drywall crew.

I was sick of all three of them. Sick of everybody, the whole world.

We were quiet, walking to the truck, and then Mike did the same thing he'd done every weekday for better than two years: fit a cigarette into his mouth and slapped his hand hard on the hood. Some kind of celebration, but being honest I was getting sick of that, too.

"Don't know why you keep this thing locked," he told me while I dug the keys out my pocket. "You drive about the ugliest vehicle I've ever seen."

I kept Lij's truck locked account of that pistol, the Luger that set under the seat like a promise you mutter to yourself, but I wasn't about to tell Mike as much. Besides, the truck wasn't all that ugly. It was a '70 Ford F-150 with a crooked fender that put you in mind of somebody's swole-up lip. Another day I might've laughed, but I was bone-tired from the work. From the work, and from something else, some queer feeling of recollecting a thing before it's happened to you. And maybe that was the lesson, the one that never quite took. You wait long enough, I mean, everybody'll let you down.

"You don't like it," I told Mike Corliss, "you can drive."

"Then I'd have to buy gas," he said.

"Yeah," I told him, "then you'd have to buy gas."

We drove down the lane the Chicago lawyer had had graded not three months earlier, that river gravel smooth as blacktop. We come up to the highway and Mike looked out at the place the road cut across cedar pine and alfalfa and he said, "What it is is, she don't know me."

I asked him who he meant. I knew who he meant.

"May don't know me," he said, smiling a little to say it, "but she will."

"That right?"

"That's right," said Mike. "We're talking destiny here. It's just like you and Syrena. You're meant to be."

I laughed, but just the same what Mike said must've worked on my mind some, maybe without me knowing it. What I'm telling you is, after a while I'd almost forgot it wasn't my idea at all.

And it surprised May when I asked her. Truth is, it surprised me.

"What do you mean, the four of us? What do you mean, double dutch?"

"You and Mike. Me and Syrena."

"You and Syrena?"

"Why not?"

"For one thing, cause you act like she's invisible when she come around. Like you don't even see her."

"I see her."

"I wonder if you do," said May. "It sure doesn't seem like it."

"Well I do. I like her."

"What about her?"

When I didn't say anything, May said: "You know what I think? I think Mike put you up to this."

She didn't even smile, saying it. Just looked at me. I knew probably there wasn't any point in lying to her.

"I don't know," I said. "I guess he had the idea."

"He had the idea and he wanted you to do the dirty work and you've done it for him. You want to be somebody's sidekick your whole life, Shelley?"

Well it was a strange question. What I was thinking: there are worse things to be than somebody's sidekick. When you are somebody's sidekick, you are something. I guess I still think so, things were a lot simpler back then.

I said, "Mike's been a good friend to me."

"I don't trust him," she said. "I don't trust Mike at all."

She chewed her lip, which is what May does when she's nervous, or afraid, or trying not to smile. I didn't know which one it was just then.

"Let him grow on you," I said. "He'll grow on you."

By the time the four of us—me and Mike, May and Syrena—had our date, it was coming up on fall. Hotter than hell, still, but the green in the trees was cracked yellow in places, and at night you thought sometimes you'd rather have a coat. Me and Mike pulled up in what we'd worked in: blue jeans and holey tee shirts. I remember how he kept fussing with that blue bandana on the way over, wiping the sweat off his forehead and setting it on the dash and then taking it up again, wiping his forehead, setting it on the dash.

"Leave that thing alone," I told him. "You're making me nervous."

May and Syrena were pulling in just as we did, and it was strange seeing my sister step out of Syrena's car, all gussied up from work. She looked an awful lot like Momma, and very beautiful all the sudden, and she looked old—hell, she was old, she'd have been twenty-four that year. Syrena didn't look awful, either. Back then she had a so-so face the makeup did favors to, very dark hair and very blue eyes.

When the girls made their way over to where we were standing, Mike didn't so much as nod in May's direction. He kept his hands stuffed in the pockets of his jeans, and his face had went pale as paper. All that big talk, I thought, smiling to myself.

I dug around in my head for something to tell them, and what I come up with was: "How are you ladies doing?"

May just give me a look: "I'm not a lady, Shelley. I'm May."

Which is by way of saying, I knew all this was a bad idea, right off the bat. For one thing, I've never much liked bars. If I drink, I like to do it in my own house, or an automobile. The Go-Go was this ramshackle kind of a joint. Pool tables with the felt coming off, concrete floors, hardly enough light to drink by. I won't tell you about the toilets in that place, cause buddy you don't want to know. It was full up that night, and I knew if we turned down the music and told every crackerjack in there to shut up, you'd hear that humming in the air meant something ugly was coming. Who knew exactly how long it'd take to get here, but it was coming. The table pushed over on its side, and the broke glass and the quiet over the bar before that wet sound of somebody's knuckles on somebody's mouth. And I'd brought May here.

But I knew we couldn't leave. We couldn't leave cause we were miles from home now. Besides, May and Syrena were already settling in on one side of the booth and Mike was handing me a ten-dollar bill: "Get a round."

Well guess who's standing at the bar when I get there? Jarvis Wicklowe and Laughton Starbuck. I hadn't noticed the company truck in the lot, which I figured meant Starbuck'd parked round the back, cause maybe he's nervous about bowling balls falling from the sky.

At first I made like I hadn't saw them, but then Jarvis stood up off his stool and come alongside of me.

"You here with that pissant?"

His breath stunk, and the words kind of slid out his mouth.

"Which pissant, Jarvis."

"Which pissant."

"I'm here with Mike, if that's what you mean."

"Figured you were," he said. He looked like he had more to tell me about that, but just then the barman come and I held up four fingers for four Budweiser beers and handed him the money. When he'd went to fetch the drinks I turned away from the bar and looked out at the room, hoping Jarvis would take a hint. But he never did.

"Jesus Christ," he said instead. "That isn't ever May."

My sister and Syrena were still visiting at the table together. Mike was standing alone, over by the pool game. Everybody was pretending everybody wasn't there.

"Boy, she look a little like your momma, don't she."

I didn't say anything. It still didn't feel right that I'd brought her.

And then it was like he read my mind: "Keep her away from that little pissant cocksucker, hear?"

I was quiet. Then I said, "Mike isn't so bad."

"Bad?" Jarvis laughed. "Who said he's bad. He's just a pissant cocksucker. You know what I seen him do th'other day? Smoking right there on the site and dropping his butts where the deck's supposed to go. I tell him, You better pick that up, Mike. And he says, What for? This deck goes up, isn't anybody going to see it."

Jarvis kept cutting his eyes between May and the pool game.

"It's the little things, is what I'm saying."

Now the barman come with the bottles of Bud and I nodded quick at Jarvis, like, Take it easy.

But Jarvis took hold my arm: "Hold on, bud. Mr. Starbuck wants to talk to you."

So I went over to Laughton Starbuck with them four bottles of beer notched into my knuckles so I had to set two of them down just to take his hand.

"I'm always glad to see you, Shelley," he said.

I thanked him. I tried to sound like I meant it.

Jarvis had trailed me back over to where Starbuck was setting, and now the boss nodded his way: "You've got a long future in this work, Shelley," he said. "That's what I was just saying to Jarvis. You've got a good mind for the work, and you work hard. I could see you—young as you are, still—I could see you making a decent enough crew foreman one of these days."

And being honest, I was a little proud to hear him speak that way. Proud, even if something in Starbuck's smile didn't feel right.

He said, "You come here with that Michael."

He wasn't asking.

"That's right," he said. "Y'all two are thick as thieves."

I said yeah we were pretty good friends.

He said, "You know him pretty well, I guess. You know what the fellow'll get up to."

Well I took my time answering him. Cause by now I figured Starbuck was trying to get me to say something I didn't mean—or else, something I didn't want to say.

"I guess I know him pretty well."

"You tell me something about Michael Corliss."

"All right."

"He got any hobbies?"

That smile had went a little sharky. I was nervous, I wanted to get back to the table.

"Hobbies?" I said.

Starbuck nodded: "Hobbies. Does he have any hobbies. Like for example. Is Mike a bowler?"

"A bowler?" I said.

"Does he bowl?" Starbuck looked at me, knew everything. "Tenpins. Strike. Spare. Gutter. A big old thirteen-pound ball."

He was watching my face real close now. Shark-grinning.

"You're asking me does Mike bowl?"

I must've played it right: Starbuck's mouth kind of twisted itself shut. After a second he begun to say more: "About five, six months ago . . ."

But then I guess he changed his mind, cause he quit talking. "Forget it," he said. "Good seeing you, Shell." He put out his hand, I shook it, I picked up the bottles, I went to find my best friend.

By now Mike was sidling up to the pool table, where a couple boys I didn't know stood in blue jeans and matching green tee shirts that read CLAYMORE-UNION EXTRACTION SERVICES. Their skin where it showed was mud-brown, so dark that the too-blue eyes almost looked like they didn't belong in their faces. Strong-looking, good-looking boys who smiled bright white when Mike took the beer I'd brung him and nodded their way:

"I'll put two dollars on this game, if Sheldon remembered to bring me my change."

They looked at me, and I handed Mike his money. After I'd racked the balls, Mike set to studying the tip of his stick. Something about the look on his face told me I'd be the one making the chitchat, and I was right. Me and them out-of-town boys got to talking, and they told how they were roughnecks, headed home from Louisiana. Said they lived up toward Clay County. Said they were stopping for the night.

That's when Mike cut in: "Stopping here? What in hell for?"

The two of them laughed. One said: "Just figured we would."

The other said, "Sick of driving."

By now Mike had that look in his eye, the one I knew meant he was fixing to do something mean or crazy, or both: "Nothing to see here," he told them. Then: "It's your break." Still he hadn't said so much as a dozen words to May so far, not that she seemed to mind. She and Syrena set there in that booth, reminding me of a couple sisters in a church pew, chaste is the word I'm looking for.

Anyway. Took those Clay County boys about ten minutes to win the first game and hardly that long to win the second one. We couldn't have been playing a half hour by the time Mike smiled and spat in the sawdust and said, "Best out of seven."

The tall one just shrugged. By then, I could tell they were a little tired of playing, but that didn't mean they were about to give us the table. And now the other Clay County boy stuck his chin out at Mike, "I guess you owe us that two dollars." And I can see he doesn't care about the two dollars, it's just he doesn't like Mike all that much, he'd rather just get it all over with: the table turned up on its side, the glass broke on the concrete floor, the fist and so on. I could feel it coming then, boy—hear that hum—and I watched a vein doing jumping jacks in Mike's neck. We were all of us a little drunk now, me and Mike and the roughnecks, but I wasn't drunk enough just yet to scrap.

"Tell you what," I said. "Let me buy you fellows a beer."

But I know better. I know better than to think it's all right, that we will leave here and them two will go to wherever they are going and us two will go home. Now we are bound to one another, tangled up in the same ugly night. Speaking of which, Starbuck and Jarvis. They're still up at the bar, standing by the whiskey bottles. From here you can watch the whole night falling apart. Jarvis looks like a cartoon drunk, swaying side to side, his eyes half-crossed. But it's Starbuck who makes you nervous. Starbuck is real still, like he's got all his muscles tensed, and the only way you know he's been drinking is his eyes, which look like a pair of hard-boiled eggs floating in blood.

"Look," says Starbuck, "it's that Corliss boy's sidekick." Meaning me, but you can't back-sass Starbuck, so I don't say anything. But when Jarvis tells me, "Pissant cocksucker," I wheel round on him and push my face close to his.

"How's that?"

And he's sober all of a sudden. Says, "I ain't talking about you. I'm talking about your buddy."

Starbuck looks happy about all this.

I wondered should I stick my hand out, tell him, See you Monday, sir. I don't know why I didn't, exactly, except somehow I knew he wasn't through with me yet. Turned out, he wasn't.

"You ever hear the one about Ray Corliss and Eli Drummond?" Starbuck wanted to know. Drummond's who wrote Momma the script for the go-easy pills, he was Dr. Drummond to me. "Ray gone out to see Eli, a checkup. You know what Ray ask him, first thing? Doc, Ray says, you got anything to drink? Eli says, Cancer patients aren't supposed to drink, Ray. And Ray Corliss says, It ain't my liver, doc, it's my pancreas."

Jarvis laughed, too loud. I smiled, cause it's Starbuck told the story, and I knew I'd better. Still I was shamed of myself, smiling.

"It's too bad," I said. "It's too bad about Mike's dad." Meaning, Ray's cancer, but Starbuck just shook his head:

"No, it isn't," he said. "What's too bad is Rose Corliss couldn't leave him until he was too sick to chase after her. That's what's too bad."

And so I come to understand why nobody'd ever fired Mike Corliss before then: nobody'd ever felt mean enough to try it. And now Starbuck pointed with his chin crossed the bar: "What I'm saying is, the apple never falls too far from the tree."

And I turned, figuring I'd see Mike tangled up with the roughnecks. But that isn't what I saw. Mike was standing over at May's table. May had her arms folded over her chest. That look on her face, like when she's trying not to smile.

Seems to me there isn't much mystery to it. Either a woman likes you or she doesn't. You come to her, pulled by the same nothing that'll make a compass point north. You talk to her, and what you say doesn't have to make any sense. You tip your mouth close to her ear. You say, Seen any swamp rabbits lately? And she tries not to smile. She tells you, You're crazy. You're just out of your mind, Mike.

That's how a man and a woman come nearer, nearer to each other. Like the beasts of the field. Forget about the pool game, the boys you were fixing to tussle with. Forget Laughton Starbuck up at the bar. Forget about your best friend, setting over at the table with his date.

"You're crazy," she kept telling me.

"I'm crazy?" I told Syrena Mayhew. "You're the swamp rabbit."

I don't know what to say about it. Some things are so simple, it doesn't do any good trying to explain them. After a while she stood up out the booth and said, "Come on, Shell." And then we went out to Syrena's car and we necked some. I knew she wanted it, but being honest with you I didn't know how to get things started.

I said, "Okay, well."

"Well what?"

In them days, Syrena had a strange sort of laugh, this sort of high-pitched explosion. You got the feeling somehow she didn't want to laugh in the first place. I kissed her on the mouth and tried not to think about it too much when she rammed her tongue between my teeth. This whole time she's just flopping and flapping under me like something at the bottom of a canoe. Arms and legs a-going. An octopus, I thought, and I remembered Mike telling me a giant squid's mouth is in its stomach. And I get her undressed and before long things are up and running and I'm shuddering and shimmying and feeding myself into her.

"Don't you gunk in me," she said, giving my arm a little bite. "Don't you even think about it."

"I won't," I told her, but I did. And then I didn't know what to say.

"Okay, well."

"Okay well what?"

I didn't know what. I tried to think what time it must be, and it seemed like it was probably pretty late. The Go-Go would close soon. And I flashed on them all gathered round the car windows and laughing and whoo-ee, boy, Starbuck and Jarvis Wicklowe and Mike Corliss and I don't know who all, everybody just gray shadows in the light off the bug lamps, blob-faces pressed up against the windows.

"What's a matter?" she said.

I was pulling up my jeans, fastening the buttons.

"Just worried somebody's liable to see."

She give out with that exploding laugh now: "Nobody'll see," she said. "Windows is fog up."

She was right. They were gray against the wet and cool of the outside. It was fall, sure. When I looked down at her, she dragged me to her lips again.

"What're you thinking about?" she said.

But how do you explain you're thinking about nothing and everything all at once?

"Where you think they went?" I said after a while.

"Who?"

"Mike," I said, "and May."

She was quiet for a second.

"What're you thinking about them for?"

Why? Cause it was occurring to me that if we'd used the front seat of Syrena's car, that didn't leave anywhere but the cab of Lij's truck. I'd find them sprawled out there, one white knee against the windshield, one foot dangling out the window. I got out of Syrena's car quicker than you could say Starbuck, crossed that lot at a dead run. I don't know rightly what I was fixing to do. I believe I would've tore May out of that truck by her hair. I would've stood over Mike, my whole body shaking. I would've reached for the Luger only I knew was tucked under the seat.

But the truck was empty, I'd locked the doors like usual, the only thing inside was the bandana Mike had forgot up on the dash. I turned and walked back toward the bar. Syrena was waiting by them great big double doors. She took my hand, smiling.

"You're crazy," she told me. "What's the matter with you?"

And I knew she was right to call me crazy. I knew my hands could kill if they wanted.

We come in right as the Clay County boys were going out. They watched me in that half-jealous, half-curious way boys do, holding the door open. "Glad to meet you," they said. I felt so mean right then, I didn't answer back.

Mike and May had parked themselves at the same booth where she'd set with Syrena, Mike had his arm over her shoulders. And I thought to myself that my sister had told me a sort of lie: there wasn't anything to be in this life but somebody's sidekick. Now Mike belonged to her, or she belonged to him. Listen good to what I'm saying: that's how this shit works, we're all of us sidekicks to somebody else, except the ones who aren't.

"Where'd you two get off to?" Mike wanted to know.

I guess I'd kind of swallowed my tongue. It was Syrena who answered him, after a while. "None of your beeswax," she told him, and boy she was right about that, wasn't anybody's problem but our own now. She was holding very tight to my hand. I didn't like it any more than I liked that laugh of hers.

Now she looked at my sister: "What're you looking at me like that for, May?"

But May didn't say anything, just moved her eyes over Syrena's face, then mine, wondering things it wouldn't have been polite to put into words. Maybe I should explain: them two weren't quite as good of friends after that night.

After a while, I asked what time it was.

Mike shrugged: "Why? You tired?"

"A little."

"I'll bet you are," he said.

Syrena's laugh. Mercy.

May said, "Shut up, Michael."

He turned to her. He looked like he was fixing to say something smart, but all he said was sorry. Then he wiggled his way closer, fit his arm tighter round her shoulders. And I knew it then, everything was going to be different, and boy was I right about that. Not even a year, and we'd both of us be fathers. Sovereign was born in April, Layla end of July.

After Syrena had got in her car and went south on sixty-three, toward West Plains, May and Mike and me piled into the truck. May set in the middle, her legs kicked over his lap to keep clear of the gearshift. I guessed she didn't know how it looked: her skirt cinched up round her thighs like she was any common whore, and that kiss Mike give her that would've had Momma turning cartwheels in her grave.

"Take it easy, Shell," he called. Then he was gone away, walking the same quarter mile to his house as always.

When May had climbed back in the truck and shut the door, I didn't say anything to her. I was too ashamed, I guess, but I don't know exactly what I was ashamed of. Or who.

It was May who talked first: "You all right, Shelley?"

I said yes, I was all right.

She said, "You looked like you were about ready to cry at the Go-Go."

There wasn't anything worth saying, so I didn't.

"Syrena's a man-eater," she said. "Guess I should've warned you."

When I pulled up to the house and May got out, I looked at the fuel gauge and seen it was at a quarter tank. Mike had left his bandana on the dash, his cigarettes, too. I looked at May. The questions were all gone out of her eyes. When I told her I'd forgot something at the Go-Go, that I had to get back there, she told me, "Come inside, Shelley. Come on inside and get you to bed."

But it wasn't all that late. The Go-Go was still open. When I got back to the bar, I could see the last of the summer moths chucking themselves against the pillbox windows. Just a few cars in the lot. And out toward the back, right where I'd figured it would be, this Chevrolet C30 with STARBUCK AND PURCHISS CONSTRUC-TION LLC wrote on the side.

I come up alongside of it. Not one chip in that baby-blue paint, and the rear fender shining like the family silver. The green light from the bar over the windshield he'd had fixed not half a year ago. I put Lij's truck in neutral and pulled up the hand brake and reached crossed the cab for the bandana and smokes. I got out and walked over to the company truck. When I'd got the mouth of the gas tank stuffed pretty good with the bandana, I fished the matches from where he kept them, wedged against the last four cigarettes in the pack. Then I lit the bandana, and up it went, burning clean and true and not too quick.

I was already back on the highway by the time Laughton Star-buck's truck went up like a Roman candle. I'd have liked to stick around to see that cocksucker's face, but I knew better.

Way I see it, it wasn't any skin off his nose: must've had that thing insured. I think maybe it would've all played right, except Cal

Purchiss and Laughton Starbuck had it out for my best friend Mike Corliss. He'd figured it was Mike who put that bowling ball through his windshield, and I guess it kind of stood to reason Mike was the one to torch the truck. Mike said he never done it, but by then his word didn't count for much. The only thing must've saved him was May telling the Law how she'd set with him all night, she knew for a fact he'd never set any fire.

Just the same, every foreman on that crew watched him close after that night. I guess Mike got plain sick of it. One day, about a month before Layla was born, Mike come to the site real calm, give his two weeks' notice: he'd just joined the marine corps, he said. And I guess it must've sounded like a good idea to everybody but me.

VII

On a road map it shows there isn't but three-, four-hundred miles between the Texas line and Missouri, but it's slow going to get there, friend, believe me. That rain fell like marbles from the sky since about Norman, froze solid just south of Wichita. Driver pulled off under a highway overpass to let the night come on. I guess it was about noon that second day he got on his intercom, "I don't know about you folks, but I'd like to get to Kansas City before 1988." And he turned the ignition and that whole bus commenced to yelling and clapping, and we ice-skated our way toward KC.

"Look," I tell Syrena from the pay phone in the station, "I can't control how fast the bus goes."

"The bus?"

"And the other thing is we hit a storm. Or a storm hit us. We were stuck on the highway I don't know how long."

I guess she doesn't know what to say to that. I guess she figures it was my fault, all of it, even if a great big sleet storm is a little out of my control. She says it's late. She says our boy's got bedtime coming up here in a minute.

"That's all right," I tell her. "Let him go to bed. I'll see him in the morning."

"I guess you will."

"I don't like putting you all out."

Now my eye catches on some blurry beard on the far side of the station, a great big fellow in a blue Kansas City Royals jacket zipped up clear to his throat, watching me with a pair of ink-black eyes. I turn, hunch myself into the phone. It is hard going to keep this much cash on you, and I haven't slept since Texas. But now I am tired, like my head's full up with sand, and I want to lay it down somewhere.

"It must break your heart," Syrena says after a while. "By the way, I don't know if you care to hear it. But I want you to know I've got pretty mixed feelings about you coming to visit at all."

Staring back at them ink-black eyes, I tell her: "Figured."

"You figured, huh?"

I hear the schoolteacher's voice in the background, and now my ex gives out with this great big sigh:

"All right," she says, "I'll ask him."

"Ask him what?" I wonder, an innocent question.

"I wasn't talking to you. Daniel wants to know do you have a place to stay tonight."

Daniel, that's the schoolteacher. I can't think why he'd be asking, so I'm not sure how to answer. I tell her, "Probably I'll find a hotel round here."

"Well I guess you can stay with us," she says, giving out with another great big sigh. "We've got a spare room."

For a while I try to think how to tell her no thank you. I say that it's very decent of them, offering. I nearly tell her I'll get a room, just the same. But then I can feel old blurry beard's eyes the other side of the station, watching and wondering and maybe guessing, too, and I tell my ex:

"Yeah, sure. I'd be very much obliged to you. I'll get a taxi. Shouldn't be too long."

"Never mind," she says. "Daniel'll come get you."

Before you get the wrong idea about him, I ought to explain that Daniel Gunham is an okay kind of fellow. I'd be lying if I told you he was my favorite guy in the whole world, but then I can think of a few who rank higher on my shitlist. Anyway I never wished him any harm. I met him years ago, back when me and Syrena was still married and living in Crockett with our boy. We lived on Pratt Street back then, the Sunnydale Apartments, and Daniel was this big old quiet fellow had the unit next to ours. This big old boy, a build like the star tailback of the high school football team, now he's running a little to fat. Them days he had a great big head of hair, a shade darker than mine but wild and curly. It was a while before I knew the first thing about him: that he was from down south Howell County, that he taught English over at the high school. Sometimes he played Creedence Clearwater on his record player. I remember once he come over and knocked on the door and asked was the music too loud. I just laughed. I said no it wasn't too loud. I said I reckoned you had to play CCR a little loud. I don't remember how he answered me, he always seemed real shy when I come round.

I didn't notice him acting funny, I didn't notice Syrena acting funny neither, cause I didn't think to notice. Hindsight, it all kind of makes sense, the way he avoided to look at me when I saw him at the apartment, or in town. But then some people, that's their way. And I didn't think twice about it when Syrena told me she was fixing to take the baby out to her parents' place in Howell County one Friday afternoon. I figured she was just going for a visit. I went to work like usual, come home, had some beers and slept on the sofa. Next morning I'm setting watching the TV and there come a knock on the door. *Cool Hand Luke* was on, the Saturday matinee on KOLR 10. I didn't feel much like getting up off the couch, so I just called: "Come on in."

Well it was the schoolteacher. He stood there next the door and looking at me with his eyes very wide and his chest puffed up a little. I liked the fellow, like I told you, but just then something kept me from getting up and shaking his hand. I didn't even offer him something to drink.

"Mr. Cooper," he said, "I'm here to tell you that I've got a new teaching position at a school in Kansas City."

Well now I was good and puzzled. Here was this boy I'd hardly spoke to, hardly knew, and what's his job got to do with me?

"Congratulations, Dan."

"That's not what I've come to tell you, though."

"Is that right?"

"No, that's not what I'm here for. She asked me to be the one to talk to you."

"Who did?"

But hell, even then it was clicking. And it kind of made sense. Since the baby, Syrena had quit working at the J.C. Penney's, spent all her days at home, alone. And a girl like Syrena next a tall drink of water like this, probably she couldn't help herself. I was thinking that even before he made his big announcement, which was:

"I'm going to Kansas City, and I'm bringing Syrena with me."

"The hell you are," I said.

Daniel said, "Mr. Cooper, I need to tell you that I'm in love with Syrena. I love her very much. I would do anything for her."

Was I angry? Well I was a lot of things.

"She's went to her momma's house," I said. "I guess you know about that."

"Yes," he told me. "That was my idea."

I felt stupid of a sudden, like the only one who doesn't get the joke. And then I was a little angry, but at the same time it was like a great weight come off me. Truth to tell, I was never the husband she wanted me to be. I guess I never really knew her, but now I had come to know her a little better.

I asked him just how the hell long it had been going on. "I've loved her for a very long time, Mr. Cooper," Daniel said. And then he explained how him and Syrena had went to high school together, and how when he'd saw her again after all them years, and Syrena just as beautiful as ever, and so on. He'd been carrying on like that half a minute before I held up my hand:

"All right," I told him. "Mercy."

And now I seemed to recollect the schoolteacher telling me he was from down around West Plains—Howell County, that is— which is where my wife's people are from. It had never occurred to me to ask had she knew him. Being honest, I'd never thought to ask her all that much. I'm sure I never made much of a husband, but sometimes that isn't anybody's fault. You just get into a thing and can't get out of it. I believe that was kind of our situation.

A few days later I come home from work and found Syrena picking up her and the baby's things. She tried to make a big scene, just a-crying and a-carrying on: "You don't even care, do you? You don't care your wife and your baby are leaving you! You never loved me, did you? You've got nothing inside of you, nothing!" And all that kind of thing. Well I kept my cool. I left and went to the bar and when I come back later that night all her clothes were gone, and so were Sovereign's, and so were the diapers and stroller and toys and so on.

After that it went pretty civil, by and large, excepting a dustup or two. We got our divorce and every month I put my child support in the mail and sent it on to their place in Kansas City. After Laughton Starbuck cut me to three days a week and I couldn't pay anymore, Syrena was real decent about it.

Pay what you can, she'd tell me in her letters back, and not a whole lot else.

So I've always figured Daniel must do all right for himself, out in KC, which I guess he does. Not that you'd know it just looking at his vehicle, though. He pulls up at the bus station in this little Toyota the color of a Shredded Wheat biscuit and about the same size. He looks very silly driving that thing, this big old corn-fed boy from Howell County, stooping to get out the driver's seat and shake my hand.

"You've lost your hair," I tell him, cause he has.

"You're looking a little rough yourself, Shell."

Which is one way of putting it. I shrug.

"No bags?"

I shake my head and press the pillowcase firm against my chest, trotting round the car to the passenger's side. I throw one last look over my shoulder at old blurry beard, still setting on the bench in the bus station where I've left him: his wooly head hooked to one side and his eyes closed and his mouth this great black O. It's strange how a thing seems less fearsome when you are going away from it, when it can't get to you.

"Well you must be a brave man," I tell Daniel when he settles in behind the steering wheel.

"How's that?"

"Buying Japanese."

But Daniel just smiles and pulls forward onto the road.

"Toyota makes a decent car," he says. "And cheap."

"They come cheap cause they break easy" is what I have to say about that.

He says they haven't had any trouble with this one, which kind of works on my nerves a little. Even if you know it isn't right to be anything but good and gentle and decent to him, a guy like Daniel will work on you that way. Maybe you can understand where I'm coming from here. Setting in his car, I can't help thinking to myself how I might've turned out like Daniel if the balls had broke a little different. I mean to say, I might've been the schoolteacher in the white collar his wife had just ironed for him, driving a foreign car. And there is a kind of ugliness in all them good manners, a haughtiness of spirit.

"Japanese," I say, kind of thinking aloud, "but you hate to see all them jobs going overseas. Am I right?"

"How about you?" is what he says instead of answering. "What happened to that slick little Ford you used to drive?"

"The EXP?" I shake my head. "Traded that in a long time ago. I was driving this Ford, a 150. But I wrecked it. This was down in Texas. About broke my jaw, too."

I told his wife this same story on the telephone in Oklahoma, but it doesn't hurt to explain again.

"I was sorry to hear it," he tells me after a long stretch of quiet.

"Yeah, well. Totaled the fucking thing, anyway. There's nothing left of it. I was lucky to get out of Texas with my life."

"Dang" is all he has to say. One thing I should explain to you about Daniel Gunham, I don't believe he's ever cussed in his life. Probably never smoked a cigarette, either, and I guess he's been drunk about once. Only thing he ever did wrong was covet his neighbor's wife.

"Well what were you doing down there?" he asks me now.

"Working for a man," I tell him, trying to make my voice sound easy.

"That right?"

"But I live out to Colorado these days. Montgrand. My buddy Mike got me work on a framing crew out there."

"Mike Corliss?" he asks, which is funny. Funny, cause I can't recollect their paths ever crossing. By the time Daniel had run off with Syrena, Mike had run off to the marines.

"That's right," I said. "Mike Corliss."

I must've sounded curious, cause now Daniel says, "Syrena's told me about him. Said you two used to be pretty tight."

"Still are. He's my best friend," I tell Daniel, and I can't keep the sadness out of my voice. Truth is, I don't know the next time I'm going to see Mike, or my sister, or the little girl who got his eyes.

"Well I believe Jack'll be about thrilled to see you," Daniel tells me now. "This came as a pleasant surprise to us."

And I try to think just who in the hell Jack is, and when I can't—I mean, when I have an idea but don't much like the idea—I turn to the man who stole my wife and my son right from under my nose and I say, "Who do you mean, Jack?"

And there must be something in my voice that worries Daniel, cause now he gives a little jump:

"Sovereign, I mean. We've started to call Sovereign 'Jack,' since John is his middle name."

I don't say anything for a while. I can guess what the schoolteacher must be thinking. He is thinking how it isn't any right of mine to say what the boy's name is, account of I haven't saw him in so long. Maybe the schoolteacher thinks he has the right to call him what he pleases. Maybe he is wrong.

"His name is Sovereign," I tell him.

"We don't mean any disrespect by it, Shelley."

And I watch him in his just-pressed shirt, driving the car he's a little too big for. But then I see sense. There's more to it than the balls not breaking my way. After all, I'd had Daniel's wife and in more ways than a few I did my square best to lose her. It's my own fault, just like Texas, and I think about my brother, who was expecting me yesterday afternoon, and I think about the two-bit junkie whore run off with Clayton's thirty-five grand, and my thoughts run along this way for a while, and I say:

"It's after Sovereign's bedtime, huh?"

I've said it for no good reason except to keep my mind away from other things.

"Sure is," Daniel tells me, sounding easier, and that hum in the air nearly gone now. "But you'll see him in the morning."

"I guess I will," I tell him. "What time he got school?"

Daniel shakes his head. "No school tomorrow, he's on a break. You two have the whole day together."

"Is that right?" I say, but the truth is I am afraid of my son of a sudden. Afraid of I don't know what, but later on it will occur to me: I'm afraid to think he might be old enough to hate me.

And Daniel just making it worse, telling me out of the clear blue, "Shelley, I'm awful glad you're here. Maybe it isn't my place to say it. But I think it's a good thing, you being part of Jack's—of Sovereign's—life. It does my heart good."

I don't know what to say to that. Truth to tell, I'm half ready to bust him in that big bald skull of his. And I nearly do it, too, but all the sudden my throat feels very dry, and when I cough it knocks something loose and I cough long and hard and it is all I can do to get my wind back. When I finally do, Daniel tells me:

"I believe you've about been through the ringer."

I don't answer him: it's none of his business.

"I guess you'll want a shower and a shave before tomorrow."

"Oh," I say, "that's all right."

"Just the same," says Daniel, "I believe you'll want a shower and shave before tomorrow."

They live about a half hour outside the city, just the Kansas side of the line. The house is bigger than I'd figured it would be, a split-frame with a new coat of paint shining under a blinky line of Christmas lights. The yard's winter-dead, but big, and Daniel's got red-and-green lights running in and among all the trees like baling twine.

Making my way on up toward the house, I tell Daniel I might need to borrow some clothes.

"Well my clothes might be a little big on you. But we've got some of Ellis's clothes up in the attic."

Ellis: that's my ex's dad, my used-to-be father-in-law. I don't believe he ever thought much of me, but I remember Ellis as a quiet, nice old fellow who knew a hell of a lot about birds. When Daniel explains Ellis died last Christmas, I'm mighty sorry to hear it. And now we come through the front door and find the man's daughter—my ex, in other words—at the far side of the room. Just setting at a table there, arms folded crossed her chest.

"Hey, Shell," she says.

"Hey, Rena."

The house smells like her cooking, which wasn't ever bad, and the furniture and everything looks new and clean. And still I am nervous to meet my son—but I know he's went to bed already. Now I feel calm and just dog-tired.

Daniel come in after me, now he steps round and walks to where she sets watching me. He bends and kisses her on the cheek.

"Well here's our guest," he says.

The light isn't too good on that side of the room and half her face is in the dark. She has a mug of something in her hand, and I can see the steam a-rising from it and curlicuing into the shadow. She is heavier in the face than she was when I knew her, and she has them puffball things under her eyes that will make a woman seem older than she is.

"Well, Shelley," she says after them eyes have run a few laps over me, "what do you think of this here?"

I never knew what to say to her. Turns out I still don't.

"You look different," she says. "You've got a beer belly now."

And sure, could be I'm a little thicker than I was five years earlier, but that isn't what she means. I just shrug at her, showing her I don't care one way or the other, she can be pleasant or not.

"I guess it's the beer," I say, but she doesn't bother smiling.

"What'd you say you were doing down in Texas? You're a carpenter down there?"

"Colorado," I say. "I'm in Colorado these days. Near to Denver."

"Thought you said on the phone you were in Texas."

"I was. That was something else. These days I'm working on a framing crew. Me and Mike."

She gives out with this sort of groan. "Should've figured." And when I don't answer she smiles up at her husband.

"Used to be, Mike Corliss was about all he talked about," she says, in that jokey voice that probably still means Watch Out. "Mike this, Mike that. When Mike run off, Shelley was fit to be tied. Weren't you, Shell?"

"How's that?" I ask her, trying to keep my voice steady.

"I mean, cause when Mike left, that just left me."

When Daniel sets his hand on her shoulder, she smiles up at him.

"He doesn't know what to say, Daniel."

But Daniel doesn't much know, either. And now she turns back to me, wants to know does a cat got my tongue. I tell her I guess so.

"So then tell us a story," she says, her voice gone nasty. "Tell me and my husband who socked you in the mouth."

And I'm grateful to Daniel when he corrects, "Not a 'who,' hon. A 'what.' This man's just been in an automobile accident."

I draw my hand over my mouth, which still smarts some: "Car wreck," I tell her.

"Car wreck," she says, smiling up at Daniel. Her eyes are glassy-looking, and she goes on in that same jokey-serious voice, "Golly, a car wreck, Daniel."

And when neither of us can think of what to say, I tell her what I oughtn't: "I was real sorry hearing about your dad, Syrena."

"Oh," she says, and lets a long quiet say everything.

"Well carpentry's hard work," says Daniel. "I framed house, summer of my junior year at Mizzou—boy, I've never been so sore."

It ain't so bad, I tell him. I swallow back a yawn, dig the palm of my hand into my eye, rubbing the sleep away.

"Jesus was a carpenter," says my ex.

"He sure was," says Daniel.

I'm already tired of her. Maybe it shows in my face, cause Syrena wonders, "How long you staying for?" and the way she says it not too friendly.

"I don't have to stay any longer than you want me to."

She looks up at Daniel again.

"Now isn't that a good guest," she says. "He'll just stay as long as we want him to. He won't put us out any, Daniel. That's very kind of him, isn't it?"

He gives her shoulder a little squeeze: "Okay, baby."

She is quiet and now looks away and when she does she looks all used up and sad. I don't like to see her like that. It's a shame about how love works: I mean, I did not mean not to love her.

"Well, Shelley."

She pushes her chair back and stands and turns to the side and now I can see why she'd not got up out of her chair earlier. Square over her hips is that swole that will make even an ugly woman a little beautiful.

"Mercy," I say and she come forward into the light. The meanness has went out of her face, she is even smiling a little: "That's all you've got to say?"

"Congratulations," I say.

"Yeah." She's quiet for a second, and then she looks over at Daniel. "You know, I believe it's easier the second time around. Jackie come two weeks late. Ten pounds, four ounces."

And Daniel's face just like a kid's: "Gol-ly," he says.

"Yeah," she tells him, laughing to say it, "golly is right." When she turns my way again, it almost seems like there isn't any anger or hurt in her look. But I know better, I know the past is still there, I know I did her wrong, or she did me wrong, but either way too much has happened. And she must be thinking the same thing, cause the meanness come back to her face after a while:

"You never did say, Shell."

"Never did say what?"

"You never did say how long you were going to be here."

She's got right under my skin and she knows it and she likes knowing it. But now Daniel cuts in, saves my ass again: "We can talk it over in the morning, baby. Right now this man needs something to eat and a shower and a shave."

And even though she looks like she might have something to say about all this, in the end she just duck-waddles over to the staircase:

"Fine," she says. "I'm going to bed. Sheldon, the guest room's in the basement. It gets cold down there."

"I'll bundle up," I tell her.

"You do that," she tells me. And stumps up the stairs.

When she's gone, Daniel fetches me up some bologna and bread and cheese. Says them two've got all this beer left over from Thanksgiving. Says do I mind putting a dent in it?

Sure, I tell him, if he doesn't intend to drink it.

"Can't stand beer," he says, shrugging them broad shoulders. "There's whiskey under the sink, too. Evan Williams. Took it when we were cleaning up Ellis's place, I don't know why. Neither one of us drink a whole lot."

Which is funny, sort of. Cause Syrena drunk like a fish back when I knew her.

"Anyway," says Daniel, nodding over to the fridge. "Help yourself."

While I eat he runs up to the attic for the clothes. I'm hungrier than I thought, I eat it all up like a dog. And I don't take my time with that beer, neither, I'm putting the last of it back when Daniel come down those stairs with a pile of Ellis's clothes under his arm.

"She never could give this stuff up," he says. "Saving it for Jack, I guess."

He hands me a green-and-black flannel and a pair of gray corduroy pants and a belt.

"He was a good man, Ellis," I say. "I guess it must've broke her heart."

"Well," he says. "Been a hard year for her."

Down in the basement, they've got a sofa that folds out into a good-sized bed. There's a shower down there, too, and he hunts up a towel and some heavy blankets and a disposable razor. After he's said goodnight and went up to his room, I go upstairs and have me another beer and hunt up Ellis Mayhew's whiskey, which is under the kitchen sink, right where Daniel said it'd be, next a big bottle of bleach. There are some plastic cups up top of the refrigerator, and I pour a little whiskey into a cup and set there with my two-step and drink a while at the table. That first one goes down so good I stand up and fetch a little more.

But then something changes my mind, I don't know what. I set the bottle down, go downstairs. I shower and shave, fussing with the bruises on my face like as if to make them go down. Then I put myself to bed. I close my eyes. I dream I'm awake.

VIII

Awake, sort of, on my hands and knees in scattered glass, and wet, and I couldn't stand. My hands tingling from where the glass bit into the palms. And so it all swayed back to me, the devil going: give, pay, the bottle breaking like a hot cinder against the back of my neck, the wall that danced a jig when I opened my eyes.

Candy the whore stood over by the dresser, where the TV and fifteen large was, just a crazy red shadow opening up all the drawers one by one by one.

"You can't do nothing," she said. "You can't do nothing."

And how words can make a thing be: suddenly I couldn't do much but watch her, then I couldn't even do that.

I don't know how long I was passed out. Long enough for her to find it. When I opened my eyes again, the whore was standing over me with the security box, and this hot ball rose up in my throat while she laughed her scrawny little ass off. I got my hands squared as she made for the door, swung my right foot toward me, not quite remembering the Luger until I seen the butt of it like a metal bone jutting out the cuff of my jackboot. My hand grabbed for it just as I catched some wild side-eyed view of her leg, the smooth slink of muscle under the skin, her knobby old foot all of a sudden about an inch from my face, then half an inch, and then my mouth exploding into a million pieces. I could hear seconds clang like great church bells in the space between my ears: You regret this, it went, you regret this, you . . .

I wasn't sure how bad it was yet, but I knew for certain that something had come loose in my mouth. A few somethings, matter of fact. I watched her through a red bubble of pain, her body moving in the way of a shadow along a wall. The gun, I kept thinking to myself: get the gun. But the greater part of me was calling out of red darkness, hollering at me to find just exactly where she had kicked my chin.

That hurt just rolled through me, just as it rolled through me that next day and the day after, just as it would for solid weeks, breaking like a wave at the top of my head, and rolling back, and back again, and breaking again. And the whole while my hand trying to solve the riddle of where exactly the jackboot was, and how to get the Luger clear of the cuff, and then finally I did.

I got square and worked the toggle, and I heard the bullet pop-slip into the chamber. She was this shadow flying against the wall. She was the color of a blood moon. I drew a bead on the moon and hauled back on the trigger.

Once. Twice. Missed.

I'm lucky, I guess. Room fourteen faced the street and the manager's bungalow, where Carter Landreau's brother-in-law would've been sitting, and I could've catched a manslaughter charge that night. I was too busted to run after her, and maybe I'm lucky about that, also. But maybe lucky is not the word. Next thing I knew, I was standing over the shitter, and all of it's coming up. My supper. The drink I'd fixed. One half of a tooth. And I stood that way for I don't know how long, a minute or half an hour, until I heard his voice:

"Good God, number fourteen, you in here?"

I knew just from the voice who it was, even if I'd never met the man. I tried calling out to Carter's brother-in-law, the night manager, explaining there'd been a mistake. But it come out in a chokey gargle, and a mean hurt stopped me short.

"Come again?" He wasn't exactly yelling now, but his voice carried just fine. "Mistake my ass. Get your ass out here, faggot."

Talk about your insult to injury. And the whole world a-rocking side to side now, the roll and tilt of it so strong I had to sort of tip myself through the bathroom door. And then I seen that son of a bitch. I guess he stood a couple, three inches taller than me, red hair chopped close upon this big cinder block of a head, eyes blue as antifreeze and a mouth custom-built for the scowl it was making. Veins and muscles all over his body, a regular Mr. Universe type. It hurt just looking at him, in more ways than one.

"The hell you doing with this thing?" he wanted to know.

In one of his hands he had what I thought might be a Colt revolver and in the other he had Lij's Luger. Fool, I thought, must've dropped it on the way to the toilet. That Clint seemed to know what he'd got his hands on, working the toggle to clear the chamber and tuck it into the pocket of some jeans tight enough you could about make the veins on his nut sack.

"Gunfight with the family heirloom, huh?" he said, shaking his head. "Look."

The Colt still trained on me, he turned and waved with his other hand toward the door.

"Look what you've done my door," he said. "Just look."

Twice, I'd shot. One of them bullets had went just over the doorknob, the other had took a good-sized bite out of the wall just over the frame. Lucky, like I told you. And yet now I could feel it,

a kind of trembling in my bones. That whore was long gone, Clayton's money with her. You want to know what it feels like, losing
thirty-five grand that isn't yours? It's a little like dying.

Well the pain come again now, kind of fwop-fwop-fwopping
through my whole head this time, and after that a numb feeling I
knew better than to trust.

"It wasn't me," I told him, or tried to.

"Wasn't you what? Wasn't you bled all over this carpet?"

He waved at the bloody glass mess I'd made—she'd made—between the beds.

"Wasn't me did it."

Any ordinary and decent person would've saw that talking was
a hardship for me, but this son of a bitch waved that Colt up to his
ear, "Come again?"

"She's the one," I said. "She did it."

"She did it." The night manager give a nasty laugh. "That's rich.
I ought to plug your lying ass right now, cocksucker."

I can still hear him laughing, and still I hurt all over with the
thought of it. I set down on the bed and put my hand against the
part of my face that didn't feel right. "Look at you," he laughed, his
footsteps crossing over to the john. When he got there he commenced to cussing me again: "Blood all over this son of a bitch!"
And then flushing the toilet, over and over: "Wonder how much
it's gone run me to clean this fucking place."

And then I believe the temperature in that room dropped another degree or two, cause now I recollected where the better part
of my money was hid. I stood up without knowing for sure what I
was fixing to do, just thinking it would feature Carter Landreau's
busted TV set and the door Clint the gorilla had left open.

But it was like the motherfucker could read my mind.

"Don't you move a cocksucking muscle, boy," he called out as he swung through the bathroom door, drawing a bead on me with the Colt. And we eyeballed each other for a few seconds that felt like a few months, and then I set down upon the bed again.

"It was her," I said. "I swear it to you."

"I don't care who did it," he answered, and then just studied me for a while, a sharky smile on his face. "I'm holding you personally responsible for the damage to this room, hear?"

Yes, I heard him. Half of Houston must've heard him.

He set the safety on his Colt and tuck it into his waist, the small of his back. And something about the way he moved, snake-quick and snake-smooth, put me in mind of my brother when he's angry, and that put me in mind of other things. The Law, for starters.

"Please," I said. "Please don't get the police mixed up in this. I'm begging you."

Clint just set there, laughing to himself: "Yeah," he said, "I guess you wouldn't want no police involved. Where's your bags at, boy?"

When my eyes just cut over to the busted TV, he laughed the louder: "Took your bags, diddinee?"

This time I didn't bother with setting him straight. Figured if he wanted to have the wrong idea about things, that was his business. I don't know. My head was all mixed up. A piece of me was thinking of what I'd do if Clint ever did call the Law, and another piece of me was thinking about the money in the TV set. And another piece of me was thinking of my brother playing Santa Claus to Layla Corliss. Which is to say I thought of that little girl laid up sick in bed, and of her father, and of the hundred dollars Mike had to pay every time he took her to the hospital.

"I'd say you got what was coming to you," Clint said.

And it didn't matter that Clint was right about that. The truth was bigger than me: I'd put us all in a jackpot, and Clint the night manager seemed to take an ugly pleasure in the thing. I could feel it while he paced the room, pure joy coming off him like steam. I knew that explaining—about Layla Corliss, about Nancy Cooper's shaking sickness—wouldn't do any good. And it was a weird secret wisdom come to me then. That I was lost, beyond forgiving or redeeming. And so I begun to pray. Dear God, I prayed, if you help me out of Texas, I promise you I'll get this money to who it belongs to. And right then there come a soft knocking at the door, and I watched my best friend Michael Corliss step quietly into the room.

For a second, we just sort of stared at each other. Me and Salvation. And then Salvation said, "Jeez Christ." He was looking at me where I set upon the bed with a pitying sort of fear in his eye. Then he turned to his brother-in-law.

"Clint," he said after some time, "did you do that to this man's face?"

"Wish like hell I had," said Clint, who I was generally liking less and less the longer I knew him. "You see what this cocksucker did to the room?"

Now Carter kind of looked around. Taking the mess in.

"We shouldn't let trash like this in here," Clint went on. "We ain't that kind of business."

And I remembered Carter telling me one, two, three times there was no guests allowed. And hadn't he tried to warn me?

Now with a little nod over his shoulder, Carter Landreau drew the door wide. Off a ways stood his wife. Mrs. Landreau was a round shape, with feathery hair the color of dust, hawky eyes, and yellow hands she brought to her puffed-up bosom.

"Well," said the woman, kind of sneery, "I guess he didn't like the cookie."

Carter Landreau turned to give her half a smile, then trained his eyes on me.

"Mr. Corliss," he said, "Carlie and I are going to come in, if that's all right with you."

I nodded, and he did like he'd said. Now he was closer, I could see his left side was empty, no hook and no mannequin hand, neither, it was just a pale stump past the cut of the white bathrobe he had on. I forgot to mention, him and the missus had on matching bathrobes.

"I'll clean it up," I tried to tell them, but the hurt snaked from my chin on up to the back of my head and coiled there. I couldn't find the words to answer Carter's wife when she begun to squawk:

"Clean what up? Clean what up?"

And drawing her little claw-hands together, as if to pray the whole world might disappear down some great drain in the sky.

"It's all right, Mother," Carter cooed.

"All right my ass," Clint said.

"It's all right," Carter said, his voice firmer now. "Mr. Corliss seems to have had an argument with somebody."

"You ought to see what he's done the fucking toilet," Clint said.

And Carter's little hen hustled past me where I set on the bed, past where her brother stood beside a row of empty coat hangers, into the bathroom. Oh Lord, she said, when she got there. And Carter followed when she begun to cry like that, and for a solid minute there was nothing but thin air between me and the door.

Most days, I wish I'd just run.

"You know who's done this, Car?" she shrieked. "That junkie in twenty-two. That's who done it. I told you, Car, saw 'em talking at the door—"

"Look here what I took off him," said Clint now, and dug Lij's Luger out the pocket of his jeans.

"Ain't mine," I said. But Carter Landreau must not've heard me. He never answered. When he took hold of the shooter, handling it about like you might a rattlesnake, I could see he didn't know what to make of a gun like that. And sure, it wasn't going to do him much good: the toggle on a Luger is hard to work, even with two hands—with just one, it would've been nigh impossible.

"Safety on?" he wondered, and when his brother-in-law give a grunt Carter set the Luger in the pocket of his bathrobe. Gosh, he said.

It was about then Clint asked aloud the question I'd been fearing to hear since I come to that hotel: "Just what the hell brings you to Houston, fourteen?" Speaking in that way of a man knows he's about to be lied to.

"Oil," I said.

"Oil," he said. "Oil."

And the hair on my neck gone up and up, and Carlene's voice gone up and up till before long she was just this mouse squeak in my ears. Carter, I can still hear her saying: Carter, Carter, Carter. And it was his mercy I must chuck myself upon.

"Listen," I said, looking at Carter Landreau dead-on. "I won't lie to you. It's like your missus told. That girl come in here, Candy, that little two-bit junkie you've got staying here. Don't think I feel too proud about letting her in the door. I ought to've known better."

I stopped talking for a second. The pain.

"She come in for a drink. Just a drink, I swear it to you. Then I tell her she'd better clear out, I'm tired. Well she doesn't like that, come after me with a bottle of something, she was too quick for me . . ."

But I'd talked too long and now my jaw felt about fit to come loose from my head, a wave rising and crashing so that I shivered with it. I held my hand up to my mouth for a second, just a-trembling all over and my eyes shut tight, and Clint the night manager set to laughing again. It was the sound of the whole world laughing.

"This man is seriously hurt, Clinton," I heard Carter tell him. "Mr. Corliss, do you think we ought to take you to a doctor?"

No, I was thinking, but I didn't say anything account of I couldn't talk. I just let my head hang down between my legs again, waiting for the world to slow up.

"Mr. Corliss?" come Carter's voice.

Hurt had turned his shape blurry, now he might've been the very likeness I'd saw behind the front desk that morning. I told him, "Don't bring no doctor in here. I've got a wife and son. I'm fixing to see them in Kansas City before too long."

The strange thing? How it turned out to be true.

"I'm trying to make things right," I told them. "Tonight has been one great big mistake."

And then I knew better. I knew I didn't mean any of it: even with this brass band playing full volume in my head, I was starting to sniff at the truth. That a piece of me had wanted things to go south all along, that this was the reason I opened the door and let the Whore of Babylon in the room. I was paying my brother back what was owing. It wasn't until later I knew I'd paid all of them back. Mike Corliss, I mean, and Layla, and May, and Nancy Cooper, and them girls. It wasn't until later it hit me: them all had paid Clayton's debt, too.

"Now Clint, Carlene," I heard Carter saying, "I believe we can come to an agreement with Mr. Corliss about what all has happened here this evening."

And I was saved again. I told him yes, that's exactly right, we could agree on something. But now the woman come forward, she come near enough she could just about touch me. She was looking down, down at the floor, shaking her head side to side.

"I can smell 'em. I can smell 'em on the air. Right here in our hotel. And it's Christmas. We're talking about a three-hundred-dollar bill for the carpet, alone."

"Now, Mother," said Carter.

She give a dainty little cough into her fist.

"This carpet cleaned isn't going to cost us less than two hundred dollars," she declared. "I'm sure of it."

"Cleaned?" said Clint now. "Replaced, more like. And that's not mentioning what's he's done the bathroom and the door. We're talking five-hundred-dollar worth of damage here."

Well Carter didn't look too sure about the figure, and I knew for a fact that it was bullshit: all it'd take for them bullet holes was a jar of spackling and a can of paint and an afternoon—hell, I'd have done it myself, if they'd let me—but then you have to pick your battles, don't you, and I knew half a grand was getting off easy. And besides, I thought to myself as a fearful moan gone through my chest, you're already thirty-five grand in the hole.

Five hundred would've been the last of Jake's severance pay, the only money I had in the world unless I could figure out a way to boost that busted TV set. I couldn't think how, though, not right then. An evil weariness had come over me. I had drunk and screwed too much. I had scrapped and fought and run around too much. I had lived too much, too much and too long, and a crazy idea split my whole head open now. Take a run at old Clint, see what happens.

Like I said, most days I wish I had.

"I can pay you," I told them. "Hell, I'll pay you three times that much. I just need to find that girl. She's run off with all the money I had on me."

Well the three of them just set there a minute, Carter's face tired and his wife's a little frightened and her brother's sharky and mean.

"Say you do find her," Clint said now. "How're we supposed to know you'll come back?"

Standing up took all the juice I had left in me. I pointed to Carter, to the pocket of his bathrobe, where the grip of the Luger was sticking up like a gray bone.

"That," I said.

Their faces were kind of like: What, exactly?

"That piece Mr. Landreau's got in his pocket belonged to my grandfather," I said. "He was in the paratroops, in the war. Took it off a Nazi captain in Cotentin. When he died, he lost about everything in this world except that shooter, and he left it to me. I come back with what I owe, you give me what's mine."

Well the night manager just stared at me. So I said, "Deal?"

"Yeah," Clint said after a long while. "All right."

"Let's shake on it, then," I told him, so we did.

And then come a quiet, the three of them waiting on me to leave. But of course I knew I couldn't. Not yet, anyway, not without that TV.

I looked over at Carter, kind of holding on to my jaw so as to put him in mind of how bad I'd been whooped. I told him, "I know I've got no right to ask you. But I wonder if you could see your way to giving me a few minutes to get my grip together."

His wife's face told me she might have something to say about that, but Carter answered, "That'd be fine, Mr. Corliss. You go on ahead."

Yet he didn't make any move to leave.

"I'd like to change out of these clothes, too, if you don't mind."

"Change, hell," Clint cut in now. I could swear he knew about the money I had in the TV set. "You just got done telling me that junkie freak run off with your bags, dint you? What you plan to change into, boy?"

"I guess your bags have been packed for you, Mr. Corliss," said Carter after a long quiet while. He talked friendly enough, but I could see plain what he meant: I should leave now, the sooner the better, and so I wondered was he against me, too? And now Carlene chimed in, said I ought to let this be a lesson to me. And I figured she was right about that, it was a lesson to me, just not the lesson she would've been thinking of.

The three of them stood over me, a midnight choir, so close I couldn't help seeing the family resemblance, sure as a bullet'll kill you, the same hateful little antifreeze-blue eyes. The world in a funhouse mirror. I hated all of them, and here's the strange thing: somehow I hated Carter Landreau most of all, though I don't know that I can explain the why of it. Do you know how kindness can curdle sometimes, turn to poison? Maybe that was it. Or maybe there is a certain kind of man, you don't know if you'd like to be him or put your hands round him. Do you follow me? Good and evil don't enter into it, that want's old as stone. I thought of him smiling down at Mike Corliss's name that afternoon, testing me, wondering was I sure I meant Claymore-Union.

"Mr. Landreau," I said, "I'm wondering do you mind I take a shower?"

And he said, "I'm not sure we can let you do that, Mr. Corliss."

The door was still open and I looked outside. There was night like a black fire swirling round a solitary streetlamp. Past the cut

of the hotel's roof, clouds like ash. I told you there's a certain kind
of man, you don't know if you'd like to be him or do something to
him. Well now I knew for sure that Carter was such a man, and I
wanted to put my hands round his goddamned neck.

"I'd appreciate it," I said. "I'd appreciate just a few minutes alone."

And he said, "I appreciate you appreciating it, but I think you'd
better leave now."

And that old white-hot ache went through me. And mercy,
how I hated him for it.

Looking for that whore was about like trying to find a grain of salt
in the sea. I cut down a side street didn't have a name, and under
the great tangle of the interstates, and I come to a neighborhood
where each house looked like the one next to it. Christmas lights
in the windows made squares of candy red and green from the
white. She was out there in one of them houses. I could feel her
sure as I felt the cold fact I wasn't ever going to find her.

She come this way, I kept thinking to myself.

So what, I kept thinking to myself.

And before long I come upon a great confabulation. People,
dozens of them, all down the white steps of a little white house and
out into the yard where a sprawly sort of cactus had been wrapped
in lights that blink-blink-blinked in the darkness. They must've
been kin, I'm thinking: men Clayton's age, and ladies May's age,
and granddaddies and their wives round as spare tires, hair blinking silver in the light. Out in the lawn, young men danced with
their sweethearts. The babies is what I remember best, though.
How they were all lined up on the stoop, watching my truck creak
down their street with them glassy wide eyes of kids up past their
bedtime.

And for a while I hunted for Candy's face among them, and then a man of about Lij's age, if Lij were still alive, lifted something out to me in a friendly way, and purple flame jumped out at me in a jaggy burst, and there come a pop-pop-pop!, and another, and they called out after my truck, all of them happy except for the ones standing near enough to make my face through the driver's side window. And I could still hear the firecrackers chattering when I pressed hard on the gas, and some boy's coyote song like: "I! I! I!"

It wasn't long after that I quit looking for her. Couldn't hardly keep my eyes open. I pulled off in a little alley not half a mile from the Seaside, under a streetlamp, and by its yellowy gloom I studied my face in the rearview.

Blood had plumb-lined from a cut over my eyebrow, into my eye and down into the stubble on my cheeks. My jaw where she'd kicked it was like a fist, clenched. And though I cleaned up the best I could with the napkins they had gave me with my hamburger, it was clumsy work and a white sound filled my head every time I touched my jaw.

Probably I slept, I don't know exactly. Half my mind had went white with hurt, the other half just turning things over, the truth of the thing hitting me like a bottle to the skull: I'd lost Clayton's money on purpose. Had wanted it gone, somehow. Why else had I let her in the room with me? And I didn't know why, exactly, and maybe I still don't. But if there was a why, I figured I must've been paying Clay back, for killing Momma. And paying myself back, maybe, for letting him do it. What I'm trying to explain here: I almost didn't go back for that money at all.

Just before dawn, something cold and unfriendly moved into Houston, and it begun to rain. I shivered in my half sleep and pulled the collar of my jacket up round my neck. I stuffed my hands in my pockets. And that's when I felt it, when I felt the key to room fourteen. They had never got around to asking me to give it back.

And I figured that key meant unfinished business. Just like Candy meant unfinished business when she wondered did I want just one drink, for Christmas. Just like Clint meant unfinished business when he took Lij's shooter from me. Just like Carter meant unfinished business when he tapped softly at my door, and Mike Corliss's eyes smiled at me in the almost-dark outside room number fourteen.

So I went back to the Seaside, to fetch my fifteen grand out the TV. Cause leaving it would've been crazy, or else that's just a man whistling in the dark.

IX

When I open my eyes, I can hear them three carrying on upstairs. I hear the boy's voice, nothing of what he's saying, but the way it rises and falls. He sounds happy, I think, sometimes I can even hear him laughing. And I lay still for a minute or two before getting dressed in Ellis's old clothes, thinking to myself what right did I have to come to this place. Maybe that is a fool's question, maybe I have every right in the world. He's my son, isn't he, even if the most I've done by way of raising him is a check every month, and after that a letter to say I can't make the child support anymore.

I'm here now, aren't I. I'm here, unless I'm just dreaming.

So I come up the stairs, feeling shy somehow at how loud these old jackboots sound on the steps, and there's my boy at the table in between Mr. and Mrs. Gunham.

He is a thin, good-looking fellow with Syrena's coal-black hair and his uncle's green eyes. Seems to me he's tall for his age, which is six, but then again what the hell do I know about it. He doesn't look glad to see me, matter of fact he looks a little afraid. And why not, I am a strange man in his house. For all I know, he hasn't saw so much as a picture of me, and him just a babe a-suckling when them two lit out for the traces.

"Hello," I say.

Sovereign kind of twists in his seat, not saying anything. It takes Syrena telling him, "Go'n say hello to Shelley." Then he kind of waves at me.

"Hi," he says, and I wonder is he old enough to hate me yet.

"I hope you all didn't wait for me to eat," I say, and I mean it, too: setting down to breakfast with this bunch is about the last thing I want to do.

"Course we waited," says Daniel, all loud and merry.

"Haven't even started cooking, Shell," says his wife, with a smile on her face I don't know what to make of.

I say I'm glad to hear it, and probably even the kid knows I'm lying. I look around, anxious to get it all over with. I can feel my boy's eyes on me the while, studying.

I turn to him. I say, "I heard you're going by Jack these days."

Sovereign doesn't answer me. Nobody does.

"If it's all right with you," I say, "I might like to still call you Sovereign. John is a fine name, I like the name John. It means God's grace, and Jack is close enough. You decide you'd like to be Jack, well that's fine with me. But I'm going to keep on calling you Sovereign, if that's all right. That was your grandfather's name, and I'd like you to have it. Is that all right with you if I call you Sovereign?"

He looks at me so long that I'm not sure he's heard what I've asked. Then he says, "My momma calls me Sovereign when I'm in trouble." And Syrena and Daniel begin to laugh, and before I know it I'm laughing a little, too. This boy has sort of took the edge off things.

"If she only call you Sovereign when she's mad," I tell my son, settling into the chair next his, "I guess I hope she don't have to call you that too much."

"Only around bedtime," says his momma. "This boy thinks he ought to stay up late as we do. Bedtime's the only time I have to call him Sovereign. Rest of the time, he's Jack."

Well I guess the kid has decided I'm all right. I haven't been setting for ten seconds before he gets down from his chair and draws up to me and asks do I want to see his dinosaurs. I tell him sure I'd like to see his dinosaurs but does he mind I get a cup of coffee first. So Daniel pours me a cup of coffee and then Sovereign waves for me to follow after him on up the stairs.

Well he has him a room all to himself, with a great big desk set under a great big bed hoisted up on a few four-bys, and stuffed animals along one wall in a neat row. The bed is made and the desk is neat, but I guess there must be about a hundred dinosaurs all crossed the carpet, all of them different colors and kinds. He tells me which ones like to eat plants and which ones like to eat other dinosaurs, and he tells me which ones swim in the ocean and which ones fly in the sky. He tells me some lived a hundred million years ago and he tells me some lived even longer ago than that.

He knows each of them by name, every last one of them.

And then he brings his hand up to his mouth, crossed his jaw. Says, "My mom said you were in a car accident."

"Yeah," I tell him.

"Did it hurt you?"

"No," I say. "I don't know. It didn't hurt at all."

He seems to think about that. I reckon he's smart enough to know I'm lying. He's smart enough not to say so, too.

After a good while Syrena calls us down to breakfast and the four of us set at the table, which isn't as strange as you might think.

Daniel's not the kind to run out of things to say, and this morning he wants to talk football.

"I guess you're a John Elway fan now," he says, maybe account of what I told him last night, that I was living in Colorado before I gone down to Texas. Truth to tell I don't much follow football, so I tell Daniel something I heard Mike Corliss say, back at the beginning of fall:

"You pay a man a million dollars to throw a football in some snow."

And Daniel smiles and says, "Bet you're glad they've got the bye."

And I say something I heard Mike Corliss say, back at the end of fall: "Bye don't mean a thing. What you want's momentum going into the off-season."

And Daniel says truer words weren't ever spoke. And then he begins to talk about the Kansas City Chiefs, and the sort of season they're liable to have next year. He seems to think I might know something about it, which I don't.

Syrena has fixed us a big plate of eggs and another plate of bacon and she even has some fine fruit salad. And I am feeling so glad to be eating, I was hungrier than I thought, so hungry I hardly pay any mind to the hurt in my jaw. Besides that, things going so smooth with Sovereign that I begin to forget myself, forget that I've got to go back to Colorado soon and tell my brother about what all happened in Texas, and I even half forget the ugliness between Syrena and myself.

I turn to Daniel: "Tell you what, buddy, she never cooked like this for me."

And this quiet ugliness goes through the room, the butter knife creaking along the butter dish, and the kid kind of looking round cause he knows something's wrong but doesn't know what it is.

After a while, he fixes his eyes on me: "Momma cooked for you."

"Yes," I tell him, "that's right." What's the use in lying.

He says, "She cooked for you when you were married."

And now I see he isn't asking or telling, either, he's kind of checking he understands the whole setup.

"That's right," I tell him, "she cooked for me when we were married, a long time ago."

I stand and get a little more coffee from the pot by the sink and let the heat go out of my face. That old saying, how it's a wise boy knows his father. And Daniel calls, "Let us know if you're going to want another pot, Shell. It isn't any trouble at all."

When we're through eating, Daniel goes to the sink and does the washing up while Syrena sets at the table with our boy and me.

"What would you like to do today, Sovereign?" she asks him.

He shakes his head, says he doesn't know.

"Yes, you do," she tells him. "What'd you tell Momma yesterday? Remember? What you told me yesterday?"

He doesn't answer.

"About going to see the gorillas."

"Go to the zoo," he says.

"That's right. Is that something you'd like to do with Shelley?"

"Yeah."

"Not yeah. Yes."

"Yes," he says.

I say the zoo sounds like a pretty good idea. Say I've never been to the zoo.

That kid just looks at me, them green eyes all buggy. Says, "You've never been to the zoo?"

It's about ten in the morning when the four of us get in the car. December and all, it's a bluebird sky and so warm outside I don't even need a jacket. Daniel gets in the driver's seat and Syrena waddles up to the passenger's seat and I help Sovereign to buckle in the back. Of course, the kid's pretty worked up about the zoo by now. Daniel drives like he talks, slow and steady as somebody three times his age, and the whole way there Sovereign tells about his favorite animals, and it seems to me like he knows as much about the animals at the zoo as he did the dinosaurs up in his room. I'm telling you, the kid keeps an encyclopedia in his head.

And by the time we pull up, I can hardly believe how smooth and easy everything is going. The four of us are getting along just fine, that smile pretty much superglued on Sovereign's face.

Then my ex twists round in her seat: "We'll meet you out here at one o'clock."

And the smile goes, and my son looks about like he's ready to mess himself. And I tell you, I know how he feels. Up until now, it hasn't hit me it's just going to be the two of us.

"Where're you and Dad going?" Sovereign asks after a while. Dad, he called him.

Syrena says, "We've got a couple errands to run."

I can see it's a load of bullshit, and smart as he is I reckon Sovereign can see it, too. They have fixed this whole thing so the two of us'll be on our own, and meanwhile that word keeps a-clanging through my head, Dad, Dad, Dad.

"It's just a couple hours, baby," Syrena says.

And what in the hell was she thinking, not warning him what was coming?

I look past the ticket booth and past the great big iron gates. There's a kind of rock wall over that way, and past it lives who the hell knows what. Monkeys or crocodiles or polar bears. An ugly fear takes hold of me, the general idea that none of this will go right: that this will turn out just like Texas. And it occurs to me now, maybe that's a piece of why it's took me so long to go and see Sovereign. I do not want to be angry with him, or disappointed, or shy. I have no right to be anything but good. And I catch this crosswise view of myself and feel chilled to my very bones.

"We can go somewhere else, you want," I tell him. "That's fine by me."

And Daniel says, "Well he likes the zoo. Don't you, Jack?"

And his momma says, "Jack likes the zoo."

And the boy give his mother one last look, and then he says, "I like the zoo."

So that's how it gets settled. We get out the car and my son doesn't make no move to hold my hand, which I don't fault him for. We walk just side by side, we walk two men condemned up to the zoo's great big iron gate, where a lady's selling tickets. Five bucks for me, two for him.

I know the gorillas is his favorite, so we go there first. Sovereign has stayed pretty quiet on the walk over, shy, I guess, but when he sees them great big silverback son of a bitches he runs up to their pen at top speed.

We set there a long while on one side of a great big glass wall and watch them shambling and strutting, moving low and slow and knuckly over the muddy straw. They have them a great big tree knocked over on its side and a couple of the females—you know they're females cause they aren't half the size of the boys—set up high in the bough fussing with one another's hair. Meantime this great big fellow is just watching them, and you can see he's got exactly one thing on the mind.

My boy stands there with his face pressed up close to the glass.

"You think they got names for one another?" I ask, just to say something. "Like gorilla names?"

"They all have names."

"What do you reckon his name is?"

"I don't know. The zoo makes their names."

"They do?"

"Yeah," he says. "Yes."

I look at that big old son of a bitch. Flint-colored eyes, his chest puffed out, that great thick head swiveling round on that great thick neck, and God help me but I think of the night manager of the Seaside.

"Clint," I say. "Some reason he looks like a Clint to me. What do you think?"

And my boy looks up at me, smiling a little: "Bruce," he says.

"Bruce, huh?"

"Bruce Wayne."

And I reckon I can see the resemblance, sure: that's Batman setting out there in the hay, fixing to clobber anybody gets on his bad side.

"Bruce Wayne," I tell him, nodding. "I believe you're right."

I don't know for how long we just stand here, watching him. Fifteen minutes, a half hour. When we leave, I look over my shoulder: "Take it easy, Bruce!" I holler. "See you next time!"

Which Sovereign thinks is pretty funny.

Next the gorillas is the elephants, then the tigers. This whole time we're playing the game where we name the animals. The biggest and meanest-looking tiger they've got come from over in India someplace. He's white as the snow and he sets up on this rock with his tail going, them yellow eyes burning holes into yours when he looks at you.

Ghost, we call him.

We don't talk about anything in particular. I have the feeling that I want to tell Sovereign something, but it's a something I can't quite fit words to. That he is a part of me, I guess, that he is as much mine as he is Daniel's or Syrena's. That there is my side of things, too: things he might learn, things I could teach him. That I wish I'd been more like Mike Corliss, who took to fathering natural and easy when Layla come round, but that I wasn't, and so I didn't.

By the time we've got through with the tigers, Sovereign doesn't seem any too shy. We come to the birdcage, great electric-colored parrots and canaries lighting up and crossed the mesh like a green fire, and chirping and singing out, happy and bright even if it's the dead of winter. My boy drifts from me, turns his head to look at this great big neon green-breasted son of a bitch from South America. And I can tell, just watching him, he's forgot I'm here— he's forgot he's here, if you see what I mean—and he stretches his arms out, this son of mine, and I watch him flying.

So what I'm telling you is, before things break bad, they almost seem like they might break good. And the first thing's the hippopotamus. The hippo lives in this pen, inside, must be account of it's the wintertime. Concrete walls with gray-green moss growing along them, about eight, nine, ten foot of brown water. You watch him through glass that must run about a yard thick. And the hippo a-setting there in the water, looking like a fly swimming in a shot of rotgut, his great big frog's eyes peeking over the surface.

There is something wicked about a zoo, and I mean the wickedness of keeping a living thing fixed in place. Cause I reckon hippos aren't any different from squirrels or mallard ducks or whitetail deer, or men, they want to roam and be free. And I'm standing there, thinking to myself this hippo must be about the miserablest-looking son of a bitch I've ever saw, when my boy pulls on my hand.

"What's his name?" Sovereign wants to know.

And I tell him the first thing to come to mind, say, "Looks a little like your uncle Clayton."

And the boy says, "Who?"

X

I try hard not to remember, and yet memory come billowing up in a sort of ashy cloud. Four, five days ago, this was, the morning I gone to pick up the dope. Walton is a good hour west of my place, up a two-lane road that twists and tilts like a snake on the business end of a pitchfork. Up, that road goes, up and up. Past Boulder and past Nederland, cinching like a great belt crossed the great potbelly of a mountain. Up, it goes, past a little one-room post office and fire station, up and up before the half-hid lane cutting crossed one side of the slope. Past the turnoff, a cattle guard and a gate, and that's where Clay Cooper lives with Nancy and his girls.

Truth to tell, I don't know where he grows it. My brother must still have the sense not to use his own acreage, and it occurred to me that morning it's federal land all round him, the Roosevelt, and probably he grew it out there someplace. Anyway, that's what I pictured, stepping out onto his lane, my brother moving quiet through piney woods with his spray can of herbicide in one hand, a twelve-gauge in the other.

Pretty country in the daytime, but at five in the morning it's just pure blue. The pale blue of a mountain and the paler blue of ice and the cold blue of spruce pine stretching up into a sky so dark it nearly run to black. Cold as a witch's knob, too. Not that I felt it much, walking up to the double-wide trailer Clay had hauled up there. Probably I was too nervous. I come up the two-by steps and tap-tap-tapped on the vinyl. Old Misty was already barking and clawing, like as if to wrecking ball that door off its hinges.

"Easy, girl," I called, but that just made it worse.

The dog's never liked me, by the way. She's a Rottweiler-Chow mix the exact shade of gray as the winterized dookie she'd left all over the fucking yard. Clay must've meant her for a guard, but I'm the only person I ever heard Misty bark at.

That's what he said after he'd hauled the bitch to the back of the house and lock her in the john.

"Swear to God, Shell," he said, "she likes everybody but you."

He was bent over double, red in the face from dragging her, sort of panting. He did not look too good, and a feeling like worry come over me:

"You took your time answering that door," I said, "dint you."

And kind of twisting his head round to look up at me, his breath still going like a fouled piston, Clayton said, "Well you come damned early, dint you."

He was awfully riled up. Said it must never have occurred to me my nieces might like to sleep past five in the goddamn morning. And I guess that's where it got started, this strange thought that visits on me now, staring into the briny water where Clayton the hippopotamus lives.

"Ain't they got school?" I wondered, which was a dumb question. Even I might've figured Erin and Aileen were on a break from school, it was two days to Christmas. And that's what Clayton explained, talking like you might to a child or simpleton. They didn't have school till January.

"Hell, I didn't know" is what I told him.

Clayton had his wind back by now, and he straightened up and glared at me. "Go on set down," he told me, poking his chin over at a card table they had in one corner of the kitchen. But I didn't feel much like being still. When Clayton went away down the hall, I dug through his cupboards for some coffee. I wanted something to busy my hands, something to keep my mind off what I was about to do, which was drive to Texas with a felony riding shotgun. I found the Folgers before long, filled the pot up at the sink and turned the switch, and then there was nothing left but to set there listening to the choke and gargle and sputter of the machine, and to watch the sun piling through the blinds, and think things over. By the time I heard Nancy's voice from down the hall, I had near changed my mind about going.

"You said you were going to talk to him," come her voice in a screechy whisper.

And now Clayton, answering: "I will. I intend to."

"Make sure you do."

It wasn't no mystery, it was me she meant. But talk to me? What about? It occurred to me they might try to renegotiate the deal, which frankly I wasn't about to. We'd already settled on my cut. Twenty-five hundred.

After a while Clayton come in the kitchen and pour us each a cup from the pot I'd made, explaining that him and Nancy wasn't expecting me so early, they were still getting everything ready. Hurry up and wait, I figured, that's typical. But I never said so, cause I was still wondering about what Nancy had told Clayton: Talk to him, she'd said. And why wouldn't she just do it herself? It was a puzzle. Clayton's face wasn't telling me much, either. He set quiet, though every once in a while he'd run his hand over his skein of hair, let out with a sigh. Then before too long we heard the sweeping sound of Nancy Cooper coming down the hallway. And then she come blinking into the light.

I tell you, I never saw that woman to look so rough. Thin as she was, she wore navy blue sweat pants might've fit her husband, and the drawstring cinched up round her waist like the tie of a Hefty bag, and holes poked in the white tee shirt she was wearing and holes in the pink bathrobe she had over top of it all. Must've been a jerkier day than usual, cause she swayed and sagged like a hobo on a three-night bender, them duffel bags with Clayton's dope, one over each of her shoulders, tilt-a-whirling.

I don't know what I said it for: "Mr. Bojangles, everybody!"

It was a cussed thing to say to somebody who can't help it. And Nancy give me a look then might've curled a dead man's hair: "Will you shut up, Sheldon?" she hissed. "Your nieces are asleep!"

Which just wasn't like Nancy, matter of fact I couldn't remember a time she'd raised her voice. To me, or anybody. I was too surprised to cut back at her, I just set there while she flame-throwered me with her eyes.

Then with her voice gone soft again, she told my brother, "Give me a hand with this, baby." But already he had stood to take the bags from her. And something about seeing the two of them that way made my heart feel heavy and slow. Clayton was gentle, slipping his finger under each strap, and in that red morning light I could see plain the lines each side of Nancy's mouth, and gathered round her eyes. Used to be she was a real fine, good-looking woman. That shaking sickness, I guess it done a number on her.

"Just don't get your ass pulled over," she told me, and turned round, stumble-bumming back down the hallway to their room. When I heard the door shut behind her, I looked at Clayton:

"What's up her snatch?"

And my brother never answered me, just opened the door and let the cold slam inside. Now I heard a yip and thump, Misty's claws against the laminate, some kind of fare-thee-well. Hurrying now, I took up the bag he'd left and followed my brother outside.

It seemed slower, walking back to my truck, and colder. Surprised me, how heavy that bag was. I wasn't about to catch a hernia, but then it wasn't light, either. And I guess that's when I begun to wonder again just how much profit Clayton was fixing to clear.

"How much is in here?" I asked him, pretty casual.

My brother said there was twenty-five in each bag.

"How much is fifty pounds worth?"

"Shelley," he said, "we been over this."

Which wasn't true, speaking strictly. We'd been over my cut, not Clayton's. And this is what I considered, passing through the gate and over the cattle guard, the slats ice-slick so I had to step careful in the jackboots. Fifty pounds, I was thinking to myself, and here they're about to ask me to take a smaller cut. I'd just about made up my mind to tell my brother to keep his two and a half grand, I wasn't driving any fifty pounds of dope crossed state lines. But then, before I had a chance:

"Something I've got to talk to you about, Shell," he said. "Nancy and me, we didn't much appreciate what you told Erin the other night."

I just blinked at him a second: "What'd I tell her?"

"When you told her mind she doesn't eat so much," said Clayton. "At Mike's."

"What're you talking about?" I asked him, though it was coming back to me by now: You'll wind up just like your daddy. And I looked at my brother, who was red in the face again, and that same something sunk in me like a stone. He was in the usual sweat pants and a tee shirt by now, a dungaree jacket, and in just that he wasn't even shivering. I knew it was all that meat on him, but it give me a strange feeling somehow, like he had a kind of power I didn't know anything about.

"I was just teasing her," I said. "That was just a joke."

"You don't talk to her that way," he said, like he didn't buy it for a minute. "You know she's barely ate since you said that?"

Well I wasn't about to point out that a little diet wouldn't be the worst thing ever happened to that girl.

"I never called her fat," I told him instead. "She isn't fat. It's just she's growing up awful quick, is all."

"Well that's exactly what I mean," said Clayton. "Twelve years old is a time a lot of changes happens for a young lady."

It took me a second to figure out what he meant. When I did, I about lost the breakfast I hadn't got round to eating.

"I'm sick of you treating them girls like they're trash," he said. "You do me like that, fine," he said. "But they've got enough to worry about without you, Nancy, specially."

I figured he must mean her shaking sickness. But then Clayton said something made me think that wasn't what he meant at all:

"Leave the girls out of it," he said. "They've got nothing to do with our thing."

He didn't look so steamed anymore, just sad, and that same queer feeling come to me. It was too honest, somehow. And the idea come to me then that my brother was a bad man, but in his own way he was a decent father.

A decent father, that is, unless you counted the five years he done in Huntsville, which as a matter of fact I did. Still, that idea troubled me. It troubled me even after I'd drove off, left Clay standing in the cold. While I drove east through Denver and south on I-25, I wasn't worried about state patrol or DEA or ATF or FBI. Instead I was thinking about that look on my brother's face when he told me to leave his girls out of it. And I was thinking about Nancy, who'd shivered and shook to bring them duffel bags in the room.

I stopped for gas at a place called Starkville, which was just about to the state line. When I'd filled up and paid the chatty SOB worked the register, I took a handful of quarters out to a row of pay phones at the edge of the lot and dialed Mike's number. A view of bald mountains. Sagey plains. A scree off the foothills I wasn't sure to call sand or snow.

It was May picked up, sounding like a kid on Christmas. I asked could I talk to Mike, but she said he couldn't come to the phone just at the moment. He was outside, May said, playing with Layla, and now she started in with the crying and carrying on: "I think Lay's turned a corner, Shelley." And I said maybe I'll call back later. And May, still kind of sniffling a little, asked was there anything she could help me with.

"No," I told her. "Don't think so. Not unless you can get me out of the doghouse with Nancy Cooper."

And though I didn't like doing it, I went ahead and told May about what I'd said to Erin Cooper that day at the Corliss place, and about the look Nancy'd gave me that might've curled a dead man's hair, and what Clayton had told me when we stood out in the cold.

"Well maybe you ought to apologize," May said, "maybe they'd appreciate an apology."

"Me," I said. "I'm the one."

"Well I don't know, Shell," May told me, and I knew from her voice she was getting tired of the conversation. "Do whatever you feel like. But I'm of the mind you don't tell a twelve-year-old girl she's fat. Those girls, life hasn't been easy for them."

"That ain't my fault their daddy's a goddamned jailbird."

"I never said it was, Sheldon." By now she was pretty sore. "Besides, I don't just mean Clayton. Doesn't anybody know how long Nancy'll . . ."

When she trailed off, I didn't say anything. There was that usual hot ball of nothing in my chest. Boy, was I getting tired of it.

"She looks all right to me," I said after a while.

May give out with a nasty laugh: "You're a doctor now? Those girls'll be younger than we were, Shelley. They'll be younger than we were when Momma died."

And some of the heat went out of me then, and I explained to May that I didn't mean them any harm, it was their father I had a beef with, and I could practically hear May's eyes rolling.

"I hate to break it to you, brother," she said, "but Clay Cooper isn't exactly Satan incarnate." She said that even though he had to feed them girls, and even though he had to take Nancy in for her checkups, and even though he had to pay what was owing on his spread, and even though he had to pay the delivery drivers—she kind of leaned on delivery drivers—still Clayton was helping with Layla's medical bills and so on.

"Well what do you think I'm doing this for?" I told her, trying to keep my voice steady. "Every last penny from my cut, I intend to give it to Mike."

"Well that's sweet, Shell," said May after a while, "but I think first you'd better get square with Mr. Lundeen."

"We are square," I said. "I already took care of that."

It was only later I figured I ought to've played dumb. Square about what, I should've said.

"Mm," said May, "well Mike'll be glad to hear it, considering it was him got you that job."

And then come that ice-queen voice on the telephone, saying I'd better feed another quarter in the slot. Before I could do it, though, I heard the line had went dead.

All the way through Texas, I thought the thing over. It would've been easy to call Clayton and Nancy up at them all's place, but I never did it. Past Amarillo a spiteful rain commenced to falling. I pulled off at a trucker joint and set there while the diesels turned with a sound like old men muttering to their dreams. I set there watching the rain slash over my windshield, and watching the drivers hustling crossed the parking lot and inside. The door was glass and through it I could see a pay phone, and I must've set in my truck a good half hour, staring at the fucking thing. And then the rain quit and I got back on the road, thinking to myself: Hell with them.

Hell with them all. And I suppose that's the way I've felt about it until just now, standing with my boy, looking at this great fat miserable son of a bitch floating in his bathtub. Cause it occurs to me: five years is how long Clayton was locked up in Huntsville, and five years is exactly how long since I laid eyes on this boy of mine.

You see what I'm saying?

XI

"Who?" says the boy, and him wondering give me that same restless feeling, cause now I remember everything I've managed to half forget. That soon I will go back to explain about the padlock I've cracked, and about the money, and about Candy and Carter Landreau. God help me.

"Your uncle," I tell Sovereign. "My brother. His name is Clayton Cooper . . ."

. . . And he happens to be expecting me at his house with fifty thousand dollars in a stainless-steel security box since two days ago: that's the part I leave out. And I don't mention the fifteen grand I've got tucked behind the couch in Daniel Gunham's basement, either, or the blood on the pillowcase it's wrapped in.

He Is Risen. See what I mean? And here He come now.

I look down at the boy: "You hungry?"

"No," he says.

"Just the same," I tell him, "I guess your momma will want me to get you something to eat."

He doesn't answer, so I say it again: "Best we get you something to eat, son."

He looks away, back toward the hippopotamus, and I can see plain enough he's in no hurry to go. After a long while he says, "Okay." Just, okay.

So we walk on over toward the restaurant, which is up front of the zoo, by the gate where a new lady's taking tickets, next the lion pen, where a great big fucking sign reads, FEEDING TIME 11:00.

Inside, the waiters are all dressed like they're on a safari, these khaki helmets and leather boots laced up to the knee. Our waiter's the kind that's a little too friendly. Rich, says his name tag, and my mug puts just the teeniest dent in his smile.

"Can I start you folks off with a drink?" Rich wants to know. He hands me a regular menu and my son a paper menu and some crayons.

"Me you can start off with a beer," I tell Rich. "I guess my boy wants a soda pop."

But before the boy can answer, the waiter's listed off about fifteen different kinds of soda, and in the end Sovereign wants an Orange Crush, his voice so small that Rich has to bend to hear it.

And somehow I get this feeling that I'm about to spoil this, that maybe I already have. But then I can't think how. When Rich trots off, Sovereign takes up one of the crayons, the pink one, and begins to draw a little circle over top of the lion they have on the kid's menu.

"A pink lion, huh?"

I haven't felt shy once since Syrena and Daniel drove off, not once, not until now. When he doesn't answer I tell him, "You pick anything you want off the menu." I tell him, "I don't care what you get. Doesn't matter what it cost, either." But he must be awfully interested in that lion, cause the kid doesn't look up to say he wants the chicken tenders.

"There you go," I say. "You get what you want."

Outside, this fat old woman and this fat old man are slugging along the sidewalk, making their way past the too-full trash cans, past the naked trees, past that fucking sign saying the lions'll get their food come eleven o'clock. What I don't like about a zoo, thinking about how those animals used to run free in the wild and now they set here in pens. They wait, they rot. You go to a zoo, you're paying to watch something die. And maybe it's Sovereign got me thinking this way, a kid'll boil the world down to the marrow.

Or maybe that's not right. Cause what I want to tell my son, what I guess I've brung him here to say, isn't simple at all. I can't boil it down to words other than these: I'm a thief, my son, and a fool, and worse than that. I am thinking of my brother setting at his kitchen table, peeking through the blinds, waiting on fifty grand he won't ever get. I think about what he'll tell Nancy, what he'll tell his girls. I think about what he'll do to me, and thinking about that makes me sick to my stomach.

I tell Sovereign, "Your uncle Clayton'll be glad to meet you."

And directly Rich come over with the beer and Sovereign's soda, and we order the chicken tenders, and when Rich has went away again I tell my boy:

"Now Clayton isn't perfect." I stretch my lips past my teeth, smiling. "He's had me pretty steamed a time or two, I can tell you. But at the end of the day, family's all you got."

But the boy isn't helping me much, he's still drawing all the animals in pink. He's through with the lion, now he's onto the zebra. And something about this bugs me. Cause a zebra has stripes, and my son is smart enough to color them in proper.

"Sovereign," I say, cause still he isn't looking at me.

Not that it matters, if he does look. By now I'm about three weeks and nine hundred miles away. I'm standing with my best

153

friend Mike Corliss and he's telling me to go easy. And I am not thinking straight, I am not thinking, I can't stop thinking.

By the time Rich come to set down Sovereign's food, the boy has worked that crayon to a little pink nubbin. He isn't even drawing in the lines now, just scribbling. And all of it pink.

"You go ahead and eat now," I tell him, but the crayon only moves a little slower, he doesn't stop scribbling and he doesn't look up at me, either.

"You go ahead and eat this food I'm paying for, Sovereign."

So he takes this bird bite of the chicken and set it down again, and he takes a sip from his soda, and it's worse than if he'd tried to give me sass.

"But then if you don't feel like eating," I say, gentling my voice now, "I don't want you to. Today, this is our day together. And I'd like you to do whatever you want. Lij was the kind liked to see a plate shine like a mirror."

But then it occurs to me, the boy doesn't know who Lij is, does he?

So me and Sovereign John Cooper are quiet, and directly he says he's feeling full and doesn't want any more. And even if he hasn't ate but half of that chicken I give Rich a wave and he come trotting over to the table and wonders have we saved room for dessert. Saved room, he says. I tell Rich I believe I'll have another beer and the young man will have an ice cream sundae and the check after that.

"You have an all right time?" I ask my son when Rich has went away again. By now Sovereign has picked up another crayon, blue this time, and now he sets in on what all he's colored in pink.

"I guess we've got to head home soon," I say. "You seen all the animals you were wanting to see?"

I've asked cause of what you might call manners: the truth is, probably we don't have time to see any animals now. Syrena and Daniel are coming soon. Before they do, I've got a phone call to make. But my boy says:

"The crocodiles."

"Crocodiles," I tell him. "Well how about next time. We're running a little late as it is, cowboy."

He doesn't have anything to say about that, and again it's worse somehow for the quiet. I want to tell him more, explain my side of things. But I cannot even tell him the truth. And it seems to me like the telling of all this is the trouble, there's too much to explain and we've got hardly any time to do it. The clock on the wall reading half past twelve, and I don't know how to fit words to the thing. I never will.

"All right, hell," I tell him. "I guess we've got time, if we hurry."

And that's all it takes, my boy lights up like a Christmas tree: like I told you, he is a good, sweet-natured boy.

I raise my hand again, wave Rich over, tell him to fetch me some quarters.

Pay phones are just outside the restaurant, in a little alcove, and just my luck this Tub-of-Guts is using one of them. I'm telling you, this boy is fat, even bigger than Clayton, in a yellow golf shirt and gray slacks that fit him about how ten pounds of manure fit a five-pound bag. Mine isn't the kind of conversation you want overheard, so I plug my hands in my pockets and wait for him to finish. But he just stands there, one hand jammed against his ear and the other hand pushing the phone against his rosy cheek, going like:

"I can't hear you, Laura, I can't hear you."

And them crocodiles aren't getting any younger. After a while he takes the hand he's had pressed up to his ear and pushes it into his mouth and coughs, and with his voice still warbly from the cough he goes: "Shut up, Laura. Shut up, Laura. Shut up." Real calm, you know, like he isn't telling his wife to shut up but saying, Come again? or, I appreciate it, or, Sure thing.

"Shut up, Laura. Shut up, Laura. Shut up, Laura."

And just when I think I can't take it anymore, just when I'm about ready to rip that phone out of his hand, Tub-of-Guts sets it down, real slow and almost careful about it, and he walks off.

So I pick up the phone and punch in Clayton's number, and the operator come on and tells me I need thirty-five cents to complete the call, and I roll one, two quarters down the slot and stand there while the line rings.

And rings.

And rings.

And rings, until I know isn't anybody going to pick up.

Well it's a pretty rotten feeling: three days I've been trying to work up the juice to call my brother, tell him what happened to his money, and now he doesn't even answer his phone. So I figure what the hell, I'm already out here I might as well give Mike Corliss a jingle, maybe him and May can pass along the message for me. So I roll my two quarters down the slot, I dial Mike's number, I stand there wondering what on earth will he make of all this.

But he's not the one who answers, May neither.

"That you, Nancy?"

I know it is. And about a year goes by before Nancy asks what I guess everybody's been wondering since the day after Christmas: "Where the hell are you, Shelley?"

"Missouri," I say.

"Missouri," she says.

And I know the time's come, that I'd better give her the whole story—Candy and the cracked padlock, and Clint the Gorilla, everything—but the head and the heart's two different things. It's like I told you, I lost that money half on purpose. And it occurs to me now, wasn't ever my place to collect on Clayton's bill. Vengeance is mine, so He says, and doesn't my brother have them girls to feed? And what have they to do with this ugliness? Nothing.

"Nance," I tell her, "I had a wreck. A bad one."

"A wreck?"

"My truck's been totaled, and I was pretty bad hurt, too."

She doesn't say anything for a beat, but just the same I can hear her wondering about the money.

"I tried calling you all at your place."

Dead. Quiet.

"I tried just now, wasn't no answer."

Still she doesn't say anything.

"Nancy?" I say.

And that's when I hear it, that's when I can hear her crying.

"Oh Shelley," she says, "oh Shelley."

And now I'm pretty well puzzled. I'm puzzled, cause you can feel the truth like a hot seed buried inside you, and somehow I just know it. Her crying's got nothing to do with the money. And suddenly the sky looks all mixed up, all swirly gray, and a wicked kind of joy goes through me.

"Clayton all right?" I wonder, not daring to hope something's happened to him, hoping anyway. "Where's Clayton, Nancy?" And her voice trembles to tell me, and it's everything she can do to quit crying long enough to say my brother is in the hospital. And there is some chorus of devils singing in the hollow of my chest now, and I'm thinking to myself, By God, Shelley, you've got away with it.

But I am a fool. Nancy says, "Layla's bad sick." Says, "They aren't sure she's going to make it, Shell."

Which doesn't set in right away, not really.

"What do you mean?" My throat's dry as tinder. "May told me she's turned a corner. Just a few days ago, just last week—"

But I'm all out of words, and so Nancy explains it to me. Pneumonia. She says that four days earlier, the day I left for Texas, Layla went outside account of the weather being a little warmer. That next day the cold come in, and that little girl set to coughing, and on Christmas day she was running a high fever. She's been laid up in the hospital since then. They're all of them there in the hospital with her: Mike and May, Clayton and the girls. Nancy just come to fetch some clean clothes, toothbrushes, and the like from the Corliss place. Them cancer drugs, that's the problem, how they'll all but poison you, how that little girl couldn't fight the sickness off like she might've, and a cough become pneumonia. And that's how death come, I guess, quiet as smoke.

"You best get here quick, Shelley," Nancy tells me. "If you're coming, you'd best do it quick."

And now a voice on the telephone is asking me for more money.

And it's true what they say about it pouring when it rains. It thunders, too, and lightning tears crossed the sky, and when I walk back in that goddamned African safari restaurant, wanting to kill or to scream or to do I don't know what, Sovereign is gone. At my table, just the beer I've half finished. The kid has lit out for the traces, and I just stand there a second, blinking, praying, Dear

God, Dear God. I catch sight of Rich jackal-smiling down at another table and hustle over to him. I take hold of his arm. "My boy," I tell him, "he's gone."

Well Rich quits smiling in a hurry. He looks down at my hand on his arm. He is afraid and he is right to be afraid, cause right now I'm feeling about crazy enough to jump in Bruce Wayne's cage.

"I haven't seen him, sir."

"Yes you have. He was my boy. He had orange soda."

Rich straightens up. Him and these country-club types at the table, all of them looking at me like Ronnie did that afternoon of hellfire. Rich says, "I'm sorry." But I know sorry's got nothing to do with it, I know he's thinking to himself he's a waiter, damn it, not a babysitter. And I know he's right, and I hate him anyway.

Somebody's hand on my shoulder. I turn round and there's the manager—Jack, says the fucking name tag—and he winces a little to see what Candy done to me. Then he pulls this face like he gives a dogshit about what's going on in my life.

"How can we help you, sir?"

So I explain how I stepped outside to use the telephone and when I come back my kid had walked off just on his own and nobody ever tried to stop him.

And Jack says, "Now let's stay calm. How long were you on the telephone?"

"I guess five minutes."

"Then he can't have gone far."

"It was probably closer to ten."

He says, "We'll find him."

But I know it wasn't any five minutes and it wasn't ten, either: I was gone a quarter of an hour, at least, between waiting on Tub-of-Guts and talking to Nancy. What I figure, it's probably enough time to crawl through the bars and go swimming with the alligators. And just like that it hits me where my son must've went to.

"Where's the crocodiles?" I ask Jack.

He points, I take off running.

I run crossed the whole zoo, hollering his name like a madman. I run past Clayton the hippopotamus and past the giraffes and birdcages and I don't know what all. Before long I come to a sign that says the crocodile exhibit's closed for renovations. Hanging over the sign, a picture of one of them, a great big son of a bitch with yellow evil eyes and teeth like the teeth of a Sawzall. You idiot, I'm thinking to myself, you worthless goddamned idiot.

When I turn back the way I've come, I walk slow. Calling his name loud as I can. Past birdcages past giraffes past Clayton the hippopotamus. Then the restaurant. And Rich and Jack are out front of the restaurant, and standing between them is Sovereign. There he is, my boy. Looking like he's fixing to cry any minute.

I don't know what I'm thinking, except that none of it is good. The world's all red and I can't get my wind. I take Sovereign by the arm: "The hell were you, the hell were you, the hell were you." Maybe you can't understand, saying such a thing but meaning it kindly. The hell were you, my son. My sweet son.

"He was in the bathroom," the manager tells me. "He was using the toilet."

Which figures, doesn't it: the boy's been sucking down that orange soda pop for a half hour.

I am too shamed to look at them. I'm too ashamed to thank them. I've brought Sovereign to the zoo, done exactly what he wanted. And when I take hold of his hand I pray to God my son will see I can't do any better than I've done, that I'm trying my hardest.

Great big clouds are rolling in from the west, iron-gray and cold-looking. It's fixing to snow, I can smell it, and while I help Sovereign on with his jacket I think how this must be the very storm went through Montgrand a day or two ago, the one that chilled little Layla Corliss to her bones.

In this killing cold, the zoo is emptying out quick. We come through the iron gates in a great herd. I want to be away from so many people at once. I want to part them like water. I want them all gone, or else I want them to swallow me whole, to crush me, to run over me like a great stampede.

I see Daniel's car off a ways. Syrena in the front seat.

She must know from the boy's face that something's wrong. When she gets out of the car, Sovereign breaks from me and hurries over and puts his arms round her. I pray to God don't let him be crying, and I'm shamed when I come closer and see that he is. I'm shamed cause I hate him for it, a little, even if I know better.

"What's the matter?" Syrena says. "What's going on?"

I'm feeling too mean to explain myself, to tell them about Rich and the crocodiles, I just plain don't have the gas.

"I just talked to Nancy," I say. "There's been an emergency."

"Talked to who?"

"Nancy. My sister-in-law. I've got to leave town tonight."

"You what?"

"I got to get back as soon as I can."

"Back where?"

"Colorado."

Syrena stands there, shaking her head a while. That look: like this is exactly what she knew would happen and just the same she can't believe it did. But I'm not in the mood for no dressing down.

"It ain't my fault, damn you," I tell her, and she kind of rocks back on her heels.

"You smell like beer," she says, pushing past me to open the back door and help our boy inside.

I get up front, next to Daniel Gunham. He's giving me a strange look, nearly angry. He hasn't got the details yet, but he knows I've done Sovereign wrong just the same.

In a quiet voice, he says, "Everything all right?"

"No," I tell him.

It's a quiet ride back to their house. Plenty of time to turn it all over in my head. That kid. The both of them. I get to thinking about the thirty-five thousand I've lost, and the fifteen grand that I know isn't mine to take. I get to thinking about how quiet Nancy was when I told her about the wreck, the question she hadn't fit words to yet: Did you take it, Shell? And I don't know, maybe there's no answer, and maybe there's nothing to do. But still you want to make a thing right.

And when we come to the house, I hustle downstairs and pull the couch clear of the wall and take the pillowcase out and take out one of the stacks and set it in the pocket of my painter's jacket. The other two I set in my jackboots, lacing the leather tight so the stacks are flush against my ankles. Ten grand, that still makes.

When I come upstairs, Daniel and my son are standing next the front door. Syrena's got a headache, Daniel tells me, she's lying down.

I nod. I say, "Well give her my best. And tell her this was a really unfortunate thing happened, I wished it weren't this way."

Daniel looks away, fixes his eyes on something behind me: "Called the bus station. Westbound leaves at four fifteen. We hurry, you'll be able to make it."

"That's fine," I say. "I appreciate all this, Daniel. I appreciate it a great deal. Everything."

He makes a face I couldn't quite call a smile. Yeah, well fuck you, too, buddy.

I turn to my son, he's studying something at his feet. I guess he must still be salty at me for yelling at him.

"Sovereign, I was very glad to spend this time with you. You are a very fine young man."

It's like somebody playing a song in the wrong key. And you know what I figure, that's me all over: some just isn't cut out to be fathers, and just the same they must be. I owe him this, don't I? A gift, I mean. Penance.

"Now I'm going to give Daniel something to give to you," I say, "for when you're a little older. It's a little bit of money. It isn't enough. I wish it were more."

There is just the quiet now, the boy doesn't know what to say, and being honest I don't believe I'd know, either.

"Tell Shelley thank you," says Daniel.

The boy says, "Thank you, Shelley."

Well. I hold my hand out and when Sovereign takes it his arm is limp as baling twine and still he isn't looking at me.

I say, "When I was a little older than you I got two pieces of advice that you'd be wise to follow. The first is, save ten cents of every dollar you make. Second is, always look a man in the eye when you shake his hand."

And I half turn for the door, thinking how it is worse for the quiet, worse how the boy says nothing. That's how we leave it.

Me and Daniel drive quiet, and when he pulls up out front of the station I say, "Well it's like I said. I have some money I'd like you to look after. It's meant for Sovereign, and I trust you to look after it."

"You bet, Shelley." He sounds tired, not thankful.

I reach into my pocket, fetch that third stack out. "This is for Sovereign," I tell the fence jumper.

Daniel just sets there, just stares at it.

"For clothes and things," I tell him. "And I'm fixing to give him this kind of thing more often, by the way."

Daniel takes the money slow, like he thinks it might try and bite him. But it is just plain old money, no evil in taking it. And maybe no evil in giving it, either.

"That's decent of you, Shelley," he says after a long time.

It's about ten after four o'clock by the time I get inside the station. When I've bought my one-way ticket to Denver, I bring the pillow-case into the men's bathroom and take a leak and set the pillowcase with my bloody pants and shirt in a big twenty-gallon trash can. Something ugly moving through me, this anger old as anything.

Anyhow, the Denver-bound's pulling in when I come out the john.

XII

And what I'm thinking about on the ride west, what I can't keep myself from thinking about: my brother in this great jumble of juniper and papaw and black oak, and the treetops rising level with the sink, and a hot Missouri sun poking red through the leaves like a nosy neighbor. I'm thinking about my brother standing there in bib overalls and jackboots, and a nasty-looking rash of new beard crossed of his great jowls. In one hand he's holding a three-gallon spray can of herbicide, in the other he's got Lij's double-barreled twelve-gauge.

"You're lucky," he says, throwing the shotgun over his shoulder. "Lucky I didn't shoot your dumb ass."

It'd been all right at first, when they let Clayton out in January of '83. I was even a little glad to see him, even if something had happened to Clay down in Huntsville, a thing you couldn't quite put into words. Now he was this great eyesore of a man in bad need of a shave, and his hair grown into a widow's peak, and about a hundred pounds heavier than he'd been when he gone in.

"Good behavior, my ass," I told him, shaking his hand for the first time in five years. "I don't believe it for a second."

And so there we stood in Lij's kitchen: Clayton and his girls, me and Lij. May and Layla showed up, too, though Mike Corliss was still in Lebanon, them days.

"Believe it, buddy," Clay said, laughing. "Five years I kept my nose clean."

I said, "Clean as you can in a jail, I guess."

"Guess so," said Clayton.

I smiled, even if that voice come snake-slithering to the back of my head and coiled up there: It's him did it, the voice said. He's the reason she's in her goddamned grave. But I knew it was too soon for ugliness, he'd just got out. So I set in the den and listened like everybody else while Clayton told stories about the other boys he'd knew inside. A fellow who could count cards, and a fellow who could make a batch of gin in a toilet bowl, and a fellow who thought he could talk to aliens.

"I guess when they let him out he's liable to head for Wyoming," I said, thinking of Richard Dreyfuss in *Close Encounters*.

And Clay just kind of set there, frowning at me cause he didn't know what to hell I was talking about. Movies come to the theater in Birch Tree a good year late, and Clay had went inside before they run that one.

"This movie," I had to explain, "a fellow hears music in his head makes him want to drive out to Devils Tower, in Wyoming. And the government don't want anybody to know, but there's aliens out there, and this fellow . . ."

And as I talked, Clay got this sleepy look in his eye.

"I guess I missed a whole bunch," he said, when I was finished.

And that voice come to me, He's goddamned right he did.

Still, that first night everyone got on okay. After a while Clay begun to tell about all the stuff folk'll get up to in prison, passing the time. He told how Saturday was the day they served spaghetti, which wasn't anything but macaroni noodles and ketchup. How one Saturday evening the boys made a sort of bet to see who could eat the most, and Clay won the bet, said he'd ate three bowls in fifteen minutes. And everybody laughed and laughed when my brother shown how he hustled over to the infirmary after, one hand over his rear like as if to hold things in place.

"Cool Hand Clay," I told him. And then I couldn't help myself: "Guess we know how you got so goddamned fat in there."

It was a joke, but I don't guess it was just that. And the room gone real quiet, except for Nancy, who give out with a groan. Clayton smiled after a while, said: "Guess so."

And that's how a cold war begun between us, winter of '83. On the face of it, everything was gravy. But then I might cut at Clay, or he might try and razz me about something. Usually it was my car, which was a slick little EXP practically fresh off the factory floor. And if it wasn't my car then it was the shirt I had on.

"The hell kind of man wears silk?" he used to ask me. Jealousy, pure and simply, cause Cal Purchiss had made me foreman on the crew, and my brother couldn't find work. He used to give this hang-dog look: "Won't nobody hire an ex-con."

"Sure," I'd say. "That's rough."

You figured it'd be temporary, him and the girls shacking up with Lij. But the weeks and months gone by and still Clayton had no kind of job to speak of, except to do all the things I'd done before I got so busy with the work. Used to be I was the one to help Lij with the calving and cutting, or mending fence. Once or twice I'd had to run off hunters, out-of-town boys who'd tracked whitetail onto the spread.

"Why can't Nancy get work?" I asked Clayton once, this was on toward spring of that year. "Wouldn't be any shame in letting her win the bread."

After all, that's what our momma had done, sort of, if you feel like looking at it that way. Me and Clay set out on the porch while the smell of liver frying swayed out from the kitchen window Nancy'd left open. She and May were in the kitchen, Lij had took the babies to Birch Tree, where they had *E.T.* running at the theater.

Still, Clay talked soft to answer me: "May's fixing to get Nancy a shift or two at Shady Vale."

That was the old folks home where May worked weekends, when Lij could look after Layla.

"She can't push it too hard, though."

More excuses, I thought to myself. Said, "And why's that?"

Clay explained they'd been over to Springfield, to see a doctor there, and this doctor had said sure enough Nancy had that same shaking sickness as her momma'd had, the jerking one I've been telling you about. Doctor said it was quick-moving, aggressive is the word I'm looking for, and that Nancy had better take it easy as she could.

But that had always bugged me a little. Nancy looked all right, near as I could tell. A little older, maybe, with one solitary silver racing stripe in her red hair. Hearing Clay speak of it, though, you'd think the doctor had diagnosed brain cancer. Pretty soon my brother was blubbering like a little child out on the porch, trying to keep his voice down so his wife and sister wouldn't hear. And I felt sorry for him, truly I did, but then that voice come coursing through me like a sickness. He hadn't troubled himself too much over Momma, had he? Five years, my brother did, but it had only took two to drive her crazy with missing him.

I watched him stuff his hand in his mouth while great rivers run down his fat cheeks: "She'll be a goddamned vegetable, doctor says."

"When?" I said. "How long?"

I didn't mean to sound hard, I just did.

"Too early to say."

"Yeah, well."

He had just about got hold of himself, but now he set in with a new round of crying. Worst part, he kept telling me, and then breaking off: Worst part, worst part, worst part . . .

"Worst part, what?"

"Worst part is, doctor says there's a decent chance the girls've got it, too."

"Like they caught it from her?" I asked him, throwing a wary look toward that smoke a-billowing from the window.

"Doesn't work like that," Clay said. "You're born with it, like blue eyes or brown hair or whatever. It's in the blood."

"So how do you know? How you find out if the girls've got it?"

"Tests," Clayton told me. "But them tests cost money."

By now he'd quit off crying and just looked tired and used up and old.

"Them girls'll be just fine," I told him, figuring he was working around to asking for a loan. Anybody with a lick of sense could tell Erin and Aileen Cooper were bound for a wicked fate, but I doubted some shaking sickness was going to factor into it. They were both of them big old long-legged things, with hair red as flame and eyes like the barrels of the shotgun my brother would lower on me, about a year later.

"What?" said Clayton, all the sudden.

I turned to him.

"This is a hell of a time for smiling," he said.

"I wasn't," I told him.

But I don't know—maybe I was. I remember him studying me for a beat longer, not saying anything, and then out of the dusky blue he told me, "I miss Momma." Just like that. He said it had hurt him, being inside when she passed. And I stood up out of that chair, just about choking on that forked tongue of mine.

"Got to go," I told him, and set off to walking toward my car at the end of the lane. And Clay called after me, wasn't I going to stay for supper? Called, "Girls'll be back soon." And I hollered back to him, loud enough Nancy must've heard me in the kitchen, that I couldn't stand liver. Hated the stuff.

I didn't see any of them for a while after that—just Lij, who I met once a week at the Majestic Café, in Crockett. I wouldn't say I was steering clear, exactly, just I didn't have much business being around Lij's spread, now Clayton was home.

That's what I told Lij when he asked, when he started throwing me suspicious looks:

"What you been up to, Sheldon?"

He called me Sheldon only when I'd done wrong. The truth is, I hadn't ever found a way to tell Lij what I'd told my best friend Mike Corliss: that my brother was at least half the reason Momma was in her grave.

I said, "Figure Clay's got everything under control over there."

"What's that supposed to mean?"

"Nothing," I told him. "Just I'd like to know how long's he fixing to stay with you."

Lij give me a sour look, muttering, "What do you mean?"

"I mean, when's he moving out?"

"You know as good as I do, this is just a temporary-type deal. Until he gets his feet under him."

"Half a year, it's been."

"I know it," said Lij, shrugging. "Doesn't anybody just jump up and give an ex-con a job."

"You sound just like him," I said. "Making excuses."

"He's good to have around sometime. These headaches I get."

"What headaches?" I wanted to know, but Lij just put his hands up, like: Forget about it. Which was like him, making molehills out of mountains.

"He thinks you're mad at him," Lij said now. "Clay does."

And maybe Lij would've smoked me out that morning but Cass Abrams walked through the door in the just-pressed khaki uniform that fit him like a burlap bag.

"What ho, Deputy Abrams," I called, like usual. "Had any triple homicides this week?"

And Cass laughed and said none that he knew of. Cass was all right, I don't care what they say about him. And the waitress laughed, too, and she come and topped off Lij's coffee, and mine, even though I'd had enough to just about curl my hair. Genine, I think her name was.

Lij was looking out the window, watching new pickups and old Buicks drift down Old Post Road like riverscum, church-bound.

"Well come through next week sometime," said Lij after a spell.

"I'll try," I said.

"Try. You've got somewhere else to be?"

"Work."

"On a Sunday?"

And that's how I come to be at Lij's house of a Sunday evening. And it's just bad luck, maybe, it being the twelfth of June. I hadn't thought much about the date, didn't even consider it until I come in Lij's kitchen and saw the box on top of the red Formica table with the cake through a square of clear plastic. You imagine? A birthday cake for a corpse. But that wasn't the only fool thing they'd paid cash money for: when I gone into Lij's den, I found everybody setting in front of a goddamned jumbo-screen TV. May and baby Layla and the Cooper girls and Clayton and Lij had gathered round, slouching and slack-jawed as holy rollers at a prayer meeting. On the screen, Richard Dreyfuss was making Devils Tower out of mashed potatoes.

"Take a seat, brother," Clay called, loud enough you wanted to reach a hand down his throat and squeeze. "Sunday matinee."

"Nice TV" is what I had to say about that.

"Passes the time."

After a while I crushed in with May and Layla Corliss on the love seat, which was against the far wall of the den and nigh cross-wise to the screen, and we all of us set watching, quiet except for my brother, who'd let out every once in a while with something that got on your nerves.

"This was the picture you was telling about—right, Shell?"

And me not answering him, just watching that great file of cars bound for the Devils Tower.

"Right, Shell?" come his voice again. "This the one about the fellow hears the music in his head, goes to Wyoming."

"Yeah," I said finally. "This is the one."

When the show was over, Nancy Cooper stood and laid out a big spread on the kitchen table: a great plate of fried chicken and macaroni salad, and then there was the cake, besides.

"Looks good, Nance," I told her, trying to play nice.

"Don't thank me," she said. "All this from the Town and Country. They got everything there now."

"Too hot for cooking," May said.

And so we each of us made a plate, the babies first and then Nancy and May and me and Lij. Then come Clayton, who took about everything we'd left. I remember standing to eat, account of there wasn't enough chairs to set in. And I remember it was May who said it first:

"Happy birthday, Momma."

And Lij gone after her, "We sure miss you, don't we."

"We sure do," said Nancy, who'd barely fucking knew her.

And I prayed, Dear God don't let Clayton say anything, but I guess He must not've heard me.

"Not a day goes by we don't think of you, Momma," said Clay, a wad of fried chicken tucked in one of them jowls like a chaw.

And it struck out of me, that voice, too quick for me to stop it.

"I'll bet you've thought long and hard," I said.

A quiet creaked through the kitchen on its tiptoes.

"What's that, Shell?" said Clayton.

"I said, I'll bet."

Figured there was no taking it back now, not that I wanted to.

"You know something about it?" Clay wanted to know.

"I know which dress we buried her in."

"Go easy, Shell," Lij said.

May looked down at Layla. She was just teeny, hardly old enough to do much but pick at the food. "This good, boo?" May kept asking her. "Int this good, boo?" Pretending it wasn't happening.

And Clay said, "Now that's one hell of a thing to hold against a man."

"I don't hold it against you," I said. "Hold what?"

By now, pretty much everybody had quit eating. Everybody else, I mean.

"They don't just let you out for whatever all," Clay said. "Not even for that."

"I wouldn't know" is what I told him.

"That's right," said Clay. "You wouldn't know a damn thing about it."

And for a while we watched each other without talking, and Lij got a sort of pinched look that before long I learned to mean one of his headaches was coming on.

"Your momma wouldn't like this, boys," he said. "She wouldn't like it at all."

So probably you figured, I didn't see much of Clay after that evening in June 1983, what would've been Momma's forty-eighth birthday. Except every once in a while Clay called on me at my place, the apartment I let on Old Post, behind the Feed and Supply. Fucker'd just walk right in, didn't even bother with knocking. While he set there trying to catch his breath, I'd razz him: You run here, Tub-o'-Guts? And after that we'd visit, just shooting the breeze about whatever all. The Cardinals, who were piss-poor that year. The plane the Soviets had shot down over the Pacific. Everything, excepting what was on our minds.

Anyway, it was from Clay I got the news, this smoke-blue evening in October:

"Guess you heard about your buddy."

"Heard what? What buddy?"

Yet my heart was humming like some hot stone bird in my chest.

"That Corliss boy you used to run with. Ain't you heard? He's coming home."

It seemed a hell of a long time, waiting. That bomb gone off end of October '83, but it was March of '84 before Mike come home. Day he got back, I wore my best suit—figured you had to, an occasion like this—brown wool sports jacket and matching slacks, a collared shirt pinstriped maroon, a tie that matched the pinstripes. And I would've wore the Italian leather loafers with the gold buckles I'd had to mail order from a shop in St. Louis, but it was March, and Mike's lane was a great mud river stretching the quarter mile from sixty-three to the front door. So I wore jackboots, tucking hem into cuff and lacing it all tight.

That spread, the old Corliss spread, was about the same size as Lij's. And like Lij's spread, you couldn't do much with the land but look at it. The timber was just junk trees, juniper and sycamore and tangly black oak. Damned pretty in the early springtime, though, with a honeydew smell to it and mist thick as down in among the trees. What they call a mountain in Austin County wouldn't pass for a hill out West, but from Mike's hitchgate you could make out where the Jacks Fork had knifed along the soft edge of the slope, where rusty limestone dropped a plumb line from the gray fuzz of the wood. Sometime I'll get to missing it so bad, it hurts.

And then it all turns sour again, then I remember how the woods broke open that morning, and how I saw that old farmhouse, and out front Clay Cooper's dookie-colored Chevrolet Nova.

I believe that was the morning I decided to get rid of my brother. Sure, once or twice it might've crossed my mind that we'd be better off without him. He's nothing but dead weight, I used to tell Lij, who never answered but to wave Genine over for another cup of coffee. And here Clay was in my best friend's house, the fly swimming in the shot glass, and his great big Rottweiler bark of a laugh the first thing I heard when I come through the door.

That house always used to give me the jeebies, by the way, even if it was Mike's. It was the same size and the same floor plan as Lij's, almost exactly, like the two come out of a kit. Yet the Corliss place looked darker than Lij's somehow, and dirtier, and always it felt a little empty. And maybe that's how come I didn't go in right away, why I stood by the front door, listening at what they were saying:

"They never could've proved it." This was Mike's voice. And though I was glad to hear it, I was afraid, too. "Cause hell," he went on, "I wasn't there!"

"So who set it?" Clay wanted to know, a smile in his voice.

"Could've been anybody, I guess. Maybe there's a boy they let go, he didn't like it—"

Right away, I knew they were talking about that night. That fire. It's funny, but me and Mike had never talked much about it. We had never wondered between us who had torched the company truck, even though we knew Mike wasn't the one. Which seems mighty queer to me now, him never bringing it up. Never accusing, I mean. For a solid week after that night, I'd smelled gasoline on my fingers.

"I's with May the whole time, then I gone home. That's what I told Abrams," come Mike's voice again. "What Shelley told him, too, but they never minded."

Now my brother said: "Shelley, too?"

"Hell yes. He vouched, too. I guess that's why Starbuck never tried to press charges, knew it wouldn't've stood up in court."

Clay laughed to say it: "Five'll get you ten, my brother's who torched that truck."

And probably he meant it for a joke, but when nobody laughed there come a wondering sort of silence. Then May said, "What's the use of talking about it now?" Even if she must've knew better.

And I wondered for the thousandth time had she ever thought

to tell her husband I'd went back to the Go-Go that night? And if she had, what did Mike think of that?

After a while Mike gone, "Well. Sheldon ain't that crazy."

"Sheldon?" I heard Nancy answer him, snickering. "Best not let him hear that."

And I remember there was something strange and cold in Mike's voice when he answered, "Hell, he don't mind."

"Well it's only family calls him Sheldon," Clay answered after a beat. "He must think you're family. Unless maybe he's sweet on you."

"Y'all hush," said Nancy. She had quit giggling by now, which somehow made it worse.

So now I gone right through the kitchen and on into the back, my jackboots thud-thudding on the old pinewood, and when I come in the room, the only thing I could hear was the whispery sound of stove-ash in the flue. The women set with the babies in front of the grate. Mike Corliss was in an overstuffed armchair opposite my brother. Neither one of them stood up.

"Well look at this," I said.

"Well look at it, Shell," said May. She was smiling, but a woman's face is easier to read than a man's and I could see her wondering how much of the joke I'd heard.

Nancy come to her feet now, that same wondering smile my sister had gave me: "Well we didn't hear anybody come in." She had to sort of shoo Clay's daughters in my direction. Probably they were a little afraid of me now. First Erin and then Aileen come and set their arms round my waist and I pat each of them on the back and said how big and pretty they were getting to be. Lies.

Finally Michael Corliss stood up from his chair and took my hand. Mike always was a little thin, but now I seen it was a different kind of thin, hard-edged and a mite sickly, the knobs of his cheekbones and his chin jutting at you when you looked at him, his nose seeming too long for the face it went with. Yet he was a fine-looking man just the same, and that jarhead cut suited him.

"How you making it, Shell?"

"I'm all right. How you feel?"

And there was something changed in his smile: "I feel good to be gone out of that place."

"I heard that." Now I nodded down at Clay: "Lij gonna make it?"

Clay laughed: "Well it's nice to see you, too, brother."

"Well is he?"

Clay must've cleared ten seconds before he answered me.

"Not likely," he said. Lij had been getting these headaches. And so I remembered what Lij had told me at the Majestic, and the pinched sort of look on his face those months earlier, and now worry crawfished through me. It wasn't too long before we found out them headaches were each an itty-bitty stroke. Barely half a year'd pass before he was nigh purple in the face, his mouth twisted like pipe cleaner, handcuffed to a bed in the county infirmary.

"He been to a doctor about it?" I asked my brother.

"Doubt it." He shrugged, knifing me with his smile. "I guess you could ask him yourself, you ever come round for a visit."

Already he was under my skin. Of course I still saw Lij plenty, once a week at the Majestic. Every week I saw Lij, and drank more coffee than I needed, and every week I called over to Cass Abrams at the counter: That no-account brother of mine crossed you yet? So I stood watching Clay for a second, feeling my mood turning sour, and then Mike's voice rang out like a shot:

"Aren't you going to shake the man's hand?" Mike laughed.

Which I did, after a second.

"Didn't know y'all were acquainted."

I'd been talking to Mike, but go figure Clay'd be the one to answer me.

"Only just met the dude," Clay said, "but he's had me in stitches since I did."

And this was a queer thing, occurs to me now, cause Mike seemed to get awful serious that year. May, too.

And now Clay was looking me up and down: "You're dressed for church," he said. "Or a shrimp trawler. I can't tell which."

And while they laughed I looked down at what I'd wore to meet Mike, the trousers a-billowing up round the jackboots. I felt silly in them fine clothes, and mad enough to spit.

Directly everybody went on into the kitchen and eat lunch. It was an empty little room with a rickety card table and folding chairs that called out in pain whenever you shifted. Dust and ash. May had made sandwiches and pork and beans and a fruit salad, though, which was pretty good eating if you could manage not to look while Clay pushed the food down his mouth.

While we ate, Mike told a little about Lebanon. He told about the beach there, and he told how the weather was like April in Missouri, not too hot and not too cold, just right. None of us had to ask if he'd ever shot his gun at anybody, he told us right away he never had.

After a while he talked about that bomb, the whole reason he come home. He said he didn't remember one whole day before the bomb went off, and he didn't remember one whole day after. He said he was glad to be alive, and we were all quiet for a while, thoughtful, and we might have stayed that way but that Clay likes to hog-tie a conversation.

"Well I guess that's how it works, iddinit?" Clay said. "The politicians run up the tab, and it's the army has to pay it."

And I cut in, before I had a chance to remember there was babies at the table, "Wasn't the army, dipshit. It was the marines."

There come a quiet I got to know a little too well that year, and then May called: "Well excuse him!" And they all laughed again, but the sound come ragged at its edges, and I left not long after I'd done with eating.

"Heard you and Clayton are at it again."

That was the first thing Lij said to me that week, when he met me at the Majestic. Before Hello, before How you making it, Shell? Before anything.

"What'd he tell you?" I wanted to know.

Lij shrugged: "Wasn't him to say it."

So I decided it must've been May, and drew up my shoulders to show it wasn't any big deal. I didn't feel much like talking about it now, but I guess Lij must've figured there are some dogs you can't leave sleeping.

"Your brother's had a rough few years, bud."

"Yeah," I said, "poor him."

"How's that?"

"I said, yeah I know."

"Look," he said after a quiet while, "I'd like you boys to bury the hatchet. As a favor to me, I mean."

And the look in Lij's eyes was changed, too, like as if he could see the ugliness in my mind, hear that voice that had hissed in my ear since that morning them years earlier. And both of us must've been remembering, me calling out to Lij, and him running in from the barn in the dawn light, and that sound that seemed to tear up and out of him. Not remembering, I mean, but living. Living it again, cause some things don't leave you. For example, Momma's face that morning, blue as the jeans I was wearing. And so I told Lij what he must've knew already, what he hadn't let himself believe yet, the thing I'd hissed to myself a thousand times: Clay was the reason Momma was gone. It was Clay's fault.

"Bullshit," said Lij, who didn't cuss. "Where'd you get that crap?"

I thought to explain to him about that hissing voice, but by now I knew better. It had never been anything but me. I was the one.

"I can understand you thinking Clayton had something to do with your momma," he begun, but now his eyes were glittering so that I had to figure out where to put mine. "You are wrong, but I guess I understand it."

But if Clay wasn't the one to blame, I asked Lij, then who the hell was?

"Blame?" said Lij. "Nobody. Your momma carried that sadness around her whole life."

And when I didn't answer, couldn't find the words to gainsay it, Lij said he could think of a few others I might put the blame on, a fair few. He said how about Drummond, he's the one wrote her the scrip in the first place? He said how about him who was supposed to help her, never lifted one little finger to do it? At first I didn't know who Lij meant. Then I did.

I said, "No reason to go dragging him into this."

"I don't intend to," Lij told me. "I'm just saying, isn't it funny, you not even thinking your father might've did something different? Might've helped her? God knows she needed it. But he never give her anything, did he?"

And that was true. John Sovereign never gave Momma anything, not even his name. Which is maybe how come I stole it, give it to my boy. But never mind that, Lij Cooper was on a roll now, his ears red as stoplights.

"But it's not him you hate, is it?" he said. "It's not that two-bit fence jumper, it's Clayton, cause you're too ignorant to know that hate and the other thing've got more in common than you think."

For a long time I didn't know what Lij meant, it didn't make sense to me. Neither did what he said next, which was:

"I hope Mike Corliss never crosses you, cause God help him if he does."

And even if I didn't understand him, just the same a shiver gone down my spine.

"I don't hate Clayton," I told Lij, lying through my damned teeth.

"I hope you don't," he said. "For your own sake. A grudge like that'll kill you, Shelley. It'll rot you from the inside."

I wondered maybe Lij was right about that. About everything. I wondered maybe Clayton was me in a funhouse mirror. But if you think wondering that made me hate him any less, you are a fool. We set quiet for a while, and then Genine come through with the coffeepot and smiled at me in the way she usually did and wondered did I want another cup.

"Had enough," I told her, so that she give me an unfriendly look.

And Lij, watching her rock back and forth on her way to jaw at the cook, said: "Tell you what. That'd help your state of mind."

I looked at him.

"What?"

"What do you think?"

When I turned to look toward Genine, she had leant up crossed the counter, her skirt hitching past the bend of her knee.

"Two years Syrena been gone," Lij said. "And this poor girl."

"What about her?"

"Yeah," said Lij. "Exactly."

Something I forgot to explain to you: Momma's old boss at the Angeline Factory had got Mike a job on the gripper line, which was the line Momma worked before she got her blues so bad. Well Mike hadn't been working there but three months before the Garment Workers' Union called strike. That was the beginning of the end, I guess. I remember the afternoon Cal Purchiss told me. Him and Laughton Starbuck bought me a beer at the Go-Go, waited until I'd finished to tell me they were cutting me to three days a week. Three days a week! Cal said he knew I'd worked hard for him all them years, just there wasn't enough work to go round at the moment.

"You're probably the best carpenter we've got," Laughton Starbuck chimed in. Probably. "Don't think we don't know it."

Well I never liked Laughton, even less after that fire I told you about, when he turned on my best friend Mike Corliss a couple years before all this. So I wasn't about to let him paint some pig's mouth red.

"There's less work," I said. "Okay, fine. So why don't you trim the fat a little."

"Trim the fat," said Cal.

"Yeah, that's what I'm telling you. You don't need everybody you've got working on that crew. Some of them is hardly working at all."

Cal just looked away, I guess he didn't want to see me make a Judas of myself, but Laughton Starbuck's ears pricked up: "How do you mean?" he said.

"Well just for starters, Wicklowe. His smoke breaks take longer'n his shift some days. And the whole time he's just jawing."

You know about that fat-mouthed SOB Wicklowe already: I guess he was salty I'd been made foreman instead of him, even if I wasn't but half his age. Wicklowe liked to back-sass and triple-guess everything I did. But when Starbuck nodded his head and told me he'd have to look into it, I was sorry for saying anything. There wasn't any percentage in ratting out the other boys on the crew, wouldn't help me any. Maybe Cal Purchiss was thinking the same thing, cause when he turned back to me he looked ashamed enough for the both of us.

"This is a temporary deal, bud," said Cal. "Just until the GWU call the strike off."

And they did call it off, but wasn't anything the same after that: the Angeline laid off half the folks they had working there, Mike included, and hired the other half back at a dollar less an hour. And couldn't anybody get a loan at the bank after that, cause the bank figured nobody'd make his payments. And so nobody needed to build, cause come fall half the houses in Austin County were empty. Within a year, the contracts drip-dropped like water from bad pipes.

But I didn't know all that, didn't know what was coming, and so when Laughton asked me did I want another beer, I figured hell with it. I had another beer, and then another few after that, and I've got a watery recollection of standing next to Laughton Starbuck while he lines up a shot, elbow cocked in the air like a cobra, the cue stick striking out:

"Now tell me true," he said. "Mike Corliss torched that truck— now, didn't he? No, no, it's all right. What're we going to do to him? What can we do to him? He don't work for us no more . . ."

And what made me to smile in his face, exactly? What made me tell him everything short of the truth?

"I'm not saying he did, Mr. Starbuck—"

"Call me Laughton."

"I'm not saying he did, Mr. Laughton, but I'm not saying he didn't."

And it was like that night, like going back to find that beautiful baby-blue truck in the parking lot, the moon hanging in the sky like the fruit you're not supposed to pick. And all the sudden you've done a thing that has no kind of sense or reason to it. Of a sudden there's a fire shouting in the night. And you're the one put it there, though you couldn't say why, just you're a little drunk and cause of an ugliness in your mind, the usual hot ball of nothing.

When I got tired of letting Laughton Starbuck beat me at pool, I drove over to see Mike Corliss. I don't know why I did, it would've been mighty late for a social call. May had left for the night shift at Shady Vale, and little Layla looked up at me with sleep in them great big baby blues.

Mike laughed, holding open the door so I could stumble through: "I think Uncle Shelley must've tied one on."

Now Mike was back home, I was over fairly often, and little Layla wasn't hardly shy around me anymore. She had her daddy's same smile when I bent down to nuzzle her.

"Well where've you been?" Mike wanted to know. "Bar, smells like."

Of course I didn't feel much like explaining it to him. Nowhere, I said, and followed him inside. In the kitchen, he filled me a glass of water from the pitcher and fetched out some bread and cheese and ham and mustard from the refrigerator. He said I ought to make myself a sandwich while he put Layla down, so I did. Then I stuffed it all back like some kind of animal, and made another. And when I'd put that one back I set there, thinking. I thought about the three days a week I was supposed to work, and how it wouldn't hardly be enough to pay what was owing on that slick little EXP, and I thought of what can come to a man when he's got nothing to do with himself. I thought about my brother, too, which was only natural.

When Mike had got little Layla to sleep I asked how my brother was making it these days. I guess I must've suspicioned something even then. Clay was all right, Mike told me. Nancy got on real well at Shady Vale, she worked weekends with May. And then Mike said something caught me a little by surprise:

"Guess they're glad to have their own place these days," said Mike.

"Place?" I said. "What place? Lij's place?"

"No," said Mike. "They've moved out. Got a place on Old Post Road."

And I just set there a while, saying the words back to Mike, waiting on them to take. But they never quite did.

"Well what'd they do that for?" I asked.

"Boy, Shell." Mike laughed again. "When it comes to Clayton, you don't know what you want."

"Well I'm just wondering how to hell he pays the rent."

"I don't know," said Mike. "None of my business. Maybe Nancy got another shift at Shady Vale."

But I figure Mike knew that was a long shot, too. He stood and gone to the fridge and took out some lemonade and pour us each a glass.

"I might pick up a shift there, too," said Mike. "Who knows. Probably it isn't such bad work, just you're indoors."

But we both of us knew there was just one job in the world for Mike Corliss, and that was framing house. And talking like that, trying to make the best of things, Mike looked so old. I still got blue, thinking about what I'd done to the company truck, and when Mike was around I always had that night in the back of my mind: the blue bandana I set in the gas tank and everything to come after. I guess it was a guilty conscience made me say it:

"I could get you a few hours on the crew, you wanted."

And now Mike showed his teeth.

"Sure," he said, "but Laughton Starbuck might have something to say about it."

After a quiet while Mike stood up and I followed him into the den and he turned on the TV. Guess what come on the screen, when the color settled? Them scientists pitching and tumbling through the desert, drawing up on the fence, shouting over the howling sand: We the first ones? I said, "They've been playing this for the past year, seems like," and Mike wondered did I want him to change it, and I said, "No, that's all right."

And we set there watching on that old couch. I was too tired and too drunk to notice the springs corkscrewing into my back until the next morning, when May come home from her shift at Shady Vale and wondered oughtn't I to be at the work site? That come later, though. Right then, me and Michael Corliss set watching in the quiet dark. The Devils Tower heaves vasty and black in the way-off, the Wyoming sky a blue like Layla's eyes were blue. Like Mike's eyes were blue.

And Mike said, "Pretty country."

And the thought washed over me in a great hot wave.

"We could go there," I said. "We could leave and go out there."

He turned and looked at me: "Permanent, you mean?"

"I don't know," I said. "Yes."

"Then what?" Mike wanted to know, but I'd run out of words. Then what, Shell? Then what? Cause Mike knew as good as I did, you can't just up and leave out of a life. There are doctors to pay off, and car loans, and a second mortgage on the farm. And there was Lij, too, looking grayer and older every time I saw him. There were the promises I'd made without even knowing I'd made them.

Mornings I'd see Cass Abrams at the Majestic Café on Old Post Road.

"Hey, Cass," I'd call out to him. "That no-account brother of mine crossed you yet?"

"Not yet," Cass laughed. "I'll let you know when he does."

I must've knew it all along, even before that morning I drove out to Lij's place and found my brother's turd-brown Chevrolet Nova in a clearing off to one side of the hitchgate. "Uh-huh," I said, stepping out onto the lane. And they was right where they had been the last time: couple dozen plants strung up along that ridge in a neat row, a sump pump rigged to pull from the cowpond. And I'd have ripped them dope plants up from the soil but a voice called out to me:

"Hold it."

And I turned, like the bad cowboy in the shootout. Except I didn't have no six-shooter. Closest thing was the Luger, under the seat of Lij's truck like always, but that was half a mile yet down the lane. With that double-barrel staring at me wide-eyed, my brother shook his head.

"You're lucky I didn't shoot your dumb ass," he informed me, a look on his face like he wished I'd give him an excuse.

But it occurs to me, the Denver-bound bus clicking along through these plains towns, each one like a cardboard cutout of the next, that luck had nothing to do with it. Cause I could've walked another quarter mile, fetched Lij's Luger out from underneath the seat of his truck. And me and Clay might've finished our business that very morning. But it didn't work out like that, cause I thought I knew a better way.

It might've worked, too, had it been somewheres else, or another man. But it was our land that whitetail buck strayed on that morning, and it was Cass Abrams ducking under barbed wire after him. And what nobody could've counted on was Lij, mule-stubborn. By hunting season, stroke had twisted his mouth up, made him to slur his words like a drunk. The Law hardly knew what he was saying, which happened to be: "It's my land, isn't it? And it's my dope growing there." And this he swore as long as it took him to die, which wasn't long at all: "Clayton's got nothing to do with it."

You've figured the rest by now, I reckon. They took everything, civil forfeiture, except what all they let us fetch from the house, which wasn't much: some of Momma's jewelry and things, and that old Formica table Mike and May drove out for, not long before they come to Colorado.

I'm thinking Cass Abrams must've pulled some strings, cause it was no trouble getting that old Ford out of the impound lot after Lij'd passed. And that Luger, too, the one they give me in a little plastic bag marked STATE'S EVIDENCE.

And I'm wondering to myself where the hell it's at now.

XIII

Bus got into Denver about three o'clock in the afternoon on January the first, 1988, account of that storm held us up some in Kansas. Inside the station, stumblebums lain out crossed the floor and a boy with a billy club made his way along the line. Nobody sleeps, he said, poking them with the toe of his boot. Nobody sleeps, nobody sleeps, nobody sleeps. Bunch of cabs was idling out front of the station and I got in one of them and the driver said where to.

About the only thing I wanted to do right then was see my best friend Michael Corliss. But I didn't know which hospital they were keeping Layla in, so I just told the cabbie to head for the Hover Place Apartments in Montgrand.

"Montgrand?" he said after a good while. "That's north. Pretty far north, matter of fact."

"Yeah, I guess it is. How much it going to run me?"

"I don't make the fare, the meter does."

"How much you think the meter'll say by the time we get up there?"

"Sixty, seventy dollars," he said.

"I'll give you fifty."

"Well." He tapped the meter to turn it off. "You're already in the cab."

I guess it didn't take him but three quarters of an hour. We shot up I-25, down 119, past the grain silo and the billboard at the edge of town, HE IS RISEN, and by the time we come to my place it was a little darker and plenty cold and the building stood out against the yellow wash of the plains and the mountains in the big purple way-off. And somehow it all felt too easy.

When we come up to Mrs. Gamliel's apartments, I told him, "Don't stop. Just ride me up past the rooms."

"Past them?"

"That's right. Past them. Drive me around the block, I want to see if somebody's here."

He rolled slow round the end of the block and I had him make a left so I could look in the parking lot. And sure enough, there was that turd-brown Chevrolet Nova.

"Keep going," I said, "never mind. Keep going. Don't stop."

"Keep going where?" the driver said. "This is Montgrand."

"It sure is. But I want you to take me to the other side of town."

I watched his head turning as he stepped slow on the gas: "Wish I'd kept that meter on," he said.

So I fetched the cash out from my boot and peeled one, two of them bills off the top: "A hundred dollars to take me to a motel."

I had him drive me to the Holiday Inn about a mile away, off Main Street. I paid for a night with one of the fifty-dollar bills and went up to my room on the second floor. Not a bad little joint, clean, and local calls free. I dialed the number for my apartment, the phone rang, then the line clicked.

I listened to his breathing, he listened to mine.

"Clayton," I said, "I know you're there."

"Where are you?" he wondered after a long while.

"Denver."

"Denver. You're in Denver."

"Yeah. Yes."

"And is my money in Denver, too?" he asked. "You're about three fucking days late, boy." And when I didn't answer him, when I didn't know how to answer him, he said he knew it he knew it he fucking knew it.

"Somebody's stole it," I said, figuring I'd make a clean breast of the thing. "Somebody's stole it, Clayton. It was a very bad run of luck I had down south."

"Stole it?" he said. He did not sound all that surprised, but that wasn't the strange part. The strange part was, he didn't seem all that mad, either. No, he sounded about like he'd just gave up.

"Somebody stole it," he said after a while, his voice flat as Oklahoma. "You stole it, Shelley. You did."

"I didn't. I swear to you I didn't."

"You're a liar." Still he was talking real calm, reasonable. "You're a liar, Shelley. Do you know what you've done? Do you know? Jesus Christ, Shelley, my wife's dying. Can't you see that? You've brought the wrath of God down on me. My girls . . ."

And when still I didn't answer him, he said he knew better than to think I cared much.

But that's the thing, I think I did care. Probably I still do. And I didn't know I was going to say what I said next until I had: "I'll pay you back, Clayton," I said. "I swear."

"You'll pay me back. With what money?"

For a second I was quiet, fussing with the cord of the phone.

I said, "I guess I'll get a job."

"What job?" he wondered. "What job is going to pay you enough to square what you owe?"

In a quiet voice I told him that twenty grand wasn't so much really when you thought about it, but Clayton wasn't having it:

"Let's not us pretend, Shelley," he said. "There was fifty large in that suitcase, and we both know it."

"Fifty?" I was trying hard to sound surprised, but it weren't working.

"I told you, but you knew better, didn't you?"

And I saw him again with the double-barrel throwed over his shoulder, said:

"Clayton"—my voice real quiet—"are you going to kill me?" And a piece of me wanting to hear him tell me yes.

"Kill you?" he said. "Kill you."

"Yes. Are you fixing to kill me?"

"Jesus Christ, Shelley."

"Well. Are you?"

"You're my brother, Shelley. You're my flesh and blood."

"Then what did you break in my house for, Clayton?"

"Break in?" he said. "Hell do you mean? The landlady let me in."

I didn't know quite what to think of that.

"But what're you fixing to do there?"

"Do?" He was quiet. Then he said, "I wanted to look you in the eye. I wanted to be looking you in the eye when you told me you'd stole fifty grand from me."

I waited, shame drip-dropping on me, icy water down my spine.

"Well it wasn't me stole it," I told him, but then that idea come to mind again, the one I hadn't been able to shake since that night at the Seaside: somehow I'd wanted it all to go south, I'd lost Clayton's money cause I wanted it lost. And I couldn't rightly blame that whore, either, cause it was me who let her in the room. I felt awful for what I'd done to those girls. I was sorry for everything. And what seems strange to me now, I never did apologize to Clayton.

"Tell you what," he said. "I should've listened to Mike."

I didn't ask him what he meant, I knew better than to think I wanted to know. But Clay explained anyhow: "When Mike heard it was you who'd be driving that dope down to Houston, you know what he said to me? I wouldn't trust Shelley with no fifty large, Mike said. Mike said, You'd best put a padlock on that briefcase, Clayton. And you know what, I believe Mike was right. I believe Mike's got your number."

I knew it wasn't true, that Michael Corliss would never say any such thing, and then I knew better. I remembered that crazy afternoon, the fire running down the mountain, the air compressor I didn't know I was fixing to rip until I had the pawn ticket in my hand.

"It wasn't me, Clay," I told him. "It's a long story, I'll tell you if you want to hear it, but here's the God's honest: somebody stole it. Right out from my hotel room."

He was just quiet, and it was worse than if he'd screamed. I never felt so low in my life. Whole hours, whole days seemed to go by, and then a strange thought come to me. I remembered what Lij had said, that morning at the Majestic Café, how he wanted us to bury the hatchet. For his sake, and ours.

"Well no use us fighting about it," I said.

Clay just sniggered: "Now he wants to make nice."

I took a deep breath, thinking how your sins don't ever leave you, thinking how they hold on tight, how they weigh you down.

"Well anyway," I said, "how's Layla holding up?"

I didn't believe Clayton when he told me she'd died. Or maybe I mean, I couldn't believe. But when I went down to the hotel lobby and found that day's copy of the Montgrand paper, there it was in the obituaries, right where Clay said it'd be:

> The congregation of the Sacred Heart of Jesus Church of Montgrand wishes to offer its deepest CONDOLENCES to the family of LAYLA BETH MARIE CORLISS. Layla's parents, our friends MICHAEL and MAY CORLISS, need your PRAYERS and LOVE at this time. Layla is survived by Michael and May, her uncles Clayton and Shelton, her aunt Nancy, and her dear cousins, Erin and Aileen. Please join us for a celebration of Layla's life at the Sacred Heart of Jesus Church of Montgrand on Saturday, January 2, at 12:00 PM.

I stayed in the Holiday Inn that night. I didn't stay cause I was afraid of what my brother was fixing to do to me, in fact I was hardly afraid of him at all. I stayed in that hotel cause of the queer feeling I got, looking out the window of my room and seeing everything I had saw a hundred times before, this time only half recognizing it: the reno we'd done in the fall, the green edges of the trees at the park down the road from my place, the Jiffy Lube, the Burger King, the grocery store. When I lay down on that king-sized bed, there was a second or two after I closed my eyes where it was like none of this ugliness had ever happened, like I was nobody, and I was still nobody when I fell asleep. And when old Mr. Death come to punch your ticket, probably there won't be anything on the other side but a kind of black nothing. In my dreams

I can see it, how it coils and flows under the earth. I got a taxi back to my place next morning. It was cold in there. Clean, too, which surprised me: I wouldn't have blamed Clayton if he'd run a blade over the recliner, or threw a brick through the TV, or fetched all my clothes out the closet and made a little bonfire on the living room floor. But he hadn't done anything like that.

My bed, too, was just like I'd made it when I left that blue-black morning not quite a week before. In the closet, my wedding suit was still hanging in the plastic from the dry cleaner. It looked fine. I knew you wanted something black for a funeral, but this was as good as I had and anyway it was clean. I was standing in front of the bathroom mirror, fiddling with the bow tie, when I heard somebody tapping at the front door. I figured probably it wasn't Clay, but still I fetched a butcher knife from the kitchen before I answered.

"Who's there?" I called.

"Mr. Cooper?" come Mrs. Gamliel's voice. "Shelley?"

I thought to myself, Shit. Cause this was January we're talking about here, and December's rent still owing.

"Hold on a minute," I called. And when I'd set the knife back in the drawer in the kitchen, I went and opened up the front door and told her come on in.

About Mrs. Gamliel, you never heard such a story of hard luck. She's German, which is the first part, she come to America with her husband and their boy in the 1930s, and meanwhile the Nazis were dosing the rest of their family and just about everybody they knew. They started out in New York but come west around the time the war started. Mr. Gamliel worked a long time at the gravel yard even though he'd worked in a pharmacy in Germany, and Mrs. Gamliel was a maid even though she'd already went to college and study art. After the war, wasn't anyplace to go home to, and their boy was growed up besides, spoke English like anybody. So Mr. and Mrs. Gamliel bought that apartment building, and they worked at keeping it up full-time, and the son went out to a university in California to study law. Well anyway, Mrs. Gamliel never did say whose fault it was, but the boy died in an automobile accident out there, and not a year later her husband had a stroke while he was cleaning the gutters, and now it's just the widow Gamliel.

I guess she's about sixty, though it's hard to tell and I never asked, this real sweet-looking lady, with very long and very brown hair with just a bit of snow in it, and a pretty face that the wrinkles didn't make any less pretty. That morning she kind of put me in mind of a little brown bird: she wore a brown scarf and a gray sweater and black corduroy pants with the cuffs rolled up past the snow boots. It was the same getup she wore every time it snowed.

"Shelley," she said, "I thought you might be in trouble. Your brother was looking for you."

She'd been here long enough you hardly noticed the accent, but it was there, sure. Thought come out taught.

"I talked to him, Mrs. Gamliel. I been held up. Saw my kid in Kansas City."

"A kid?"

"A son. My son."

She smiled, said, "I didn't know you had children, Shelley." But I wasn't about to bite on that one, not just then I wasn't.

"If you give me just a minute, Mrs. Gamliel, I'll get you your rent money."

She shook her head. That wasn't why she'd come, she said. She didn't mind about the rent being late, she'd just wanted to see how I was doing. I told her I was fine, you know, it was just that I'd been busy. And she studied me while I talked, her arms folded over her chest and the look in her eyes like she half expected me to grow wings and fly off any second now.

"Shelley," she said when I was done, "are you going to a wedding?"

"No."

"Then you are wearing this suit for what reason?"

I looked down, and all the sudden the baby blue was bright enough to hurt my eyes.

"I'm going to a funeral," I said.

"A funeral? Oh, dear. Whose funeral?"

I couldn't get the words out just then, so I told her to wait a minute and then I went back to my room and fetch the cash out from behind my dresser. I took four bills from the middle of the stack and thought a minute and took out eight more. That was three months' rent. When I'd got back to the TV room, I explained how I wasn't sure when I was going to be able to pay her next.

She looked at the money for a while like she wasn't going to take it, so I kind of shook the bills at her until she did. Then she said, "Shelley, who has died?"

And that's how she got it out of me, and the world going slant and blurry while my hand shook as if to give her the money I'd already gave her. And Mrs. Gamliel put her little wings round me and hold me close, and that's how we were for a while, mercy, and when she let me loose, she said something along the lines of, I'm sorry Shelley, but I can't let you go to the funeral dressed like this.

I told her, "This is the only suit I got."

She held up a finger, turned, and went away down the steps.

When she come back a couple minutes later she had a black bag with her. Inside the bag was a fine suit, charcoal-colored, and it looked about like it just come out the store. I don't like to take charity, but she wouldn't let me alone until I'd went to my room in the back and try it on.

I tell you, it was like that suit was tailor-made for me. Not too tight in the shoulders, and it didn't bag at the knees any, and the leg ended just the back of my socks.

"Shoes," said Mrs. Gamliel. "What size are you, Shelley?"

And when I told her she went off again downstairs, to her place, so I walked back to the bedroom and fetch the two stacks of bills and set one each in the inside pockets of the suit jacket. After I'd checked in the mirror to make sure them stacks didn't show, I set on the couch in the fine suit, feeling pretty strange. Cause maybe they were her boy's or maybe they were her husband's but either way you cut it I'm in a dead man's clothes. When she come back she had a pair of black socks and a pair of black shoes buffed about so you could see your face in them. I never heard whose they were, and I never heard who the suit belonged to. But I tell you, we could've been twins.

I did a turn in the shoes and Mrs. Gamliel looked mighty pleased with herself. I said I appreciated it, that I didn't have any idea how I was going to pay her back. That was the truth, too, I didn't have any idea: I was fixing to give every penny I had left to my best friend Michael Corliss.

It was snowing now, a heavy and gray and ugly kind of a snow, so Mrs. Gamliel said she'd give me a lift to the church. I didn't like asking her, the church was near enough I could've walked, but them fine shoes I had on. She drives a dually-wide Ford, and it set high enough I had to hold to her hand to keep her steady when she climbed into the cab.

"Such a gentleman," she said, and in them clothes I almost didn't know better.

She backed out of the apartment lot, real slow and careful-like, twisting and turning in the driver's seat to see out the back window. After a good while she backed out onto the main road and tugged the gearshift into drive. But before she give it any gas, she smiled over to me:

"Please put on your seat belt. We wouldn't want anything to happen to your face."

And I saw what she was getting at, I still looked pretty rough: the bruises had went down some, they were more pink than purple now, but there was that tooth.

We drove and the snow come down, heavy and gray and thick even though off toward the plains the sunlight was cutting through the clouds at a slant. The church was about a half mile south of my place, and we made for that light, and all the while the snow was a-sifting and a-whirling down.

Mrs. Gamliel said, "I think Colorado is very beautiful, don't you?"

I told her, "Well yes I do."

And after that it was so quiet and almost peaceful that I half forgot where I was going, and I was sorry when she pulled up out front of the church steps.

I remember Mrs. Gamliel stopped me when I tugged open the door and stepped out into the wet.

"Shelley," she said, "why don't you come and visit with me sometime?"

"Sure," I said. "I'll do that, Mrs. Gamliel."

"It seems to me that you have a great deal on your mind." When I didn't answer her, she went on:

"You're welcome anytime, of course."

"I'll come see you," I said. "I promise."

But she just set there, nodding like she knew better.

When I come through the doors the ministration had already begun so I stood against the far wall. I could see Mike and May in the pew up front. I saw Clay next my sister, Nancy and the girls next him. The boys from Lundeen's crew were in among the crowd. Jake Lundeen himself set right behind Clayton, alone. Eric from Boston was there with his wife, and I saw Hector and Luis there with their families.

I didn't listen to the sermon too close. There was a whole mess of crying and carrying on in there. The whole congregation, too, not just my sister, account of Layla being such a sweet and good-natured little girl. And I remember May letting go with a great big wail so that the minister had to leave off what he was saying. He looked about like every preacher-man you ever saw: tall, with wire-rimmed glasses and a head bald as an egg.

And I didn't go up for visitation, either, remembering a little too good what the mortician did to Momma, you don't like to see your niece made up like a five-year-old tart. Every funeral ought to be close-casket, you want my candid opinion.

After the visitation they had a reception-type deal in a room just off the sermon hall. The congregation had about outdid itself. There was a great big pot roast and enough potatoes and macaroni salad to feed the marine corps. There wasn't any beer, it being a church, but there was a great big cooler full up with soda pop.

I was standing there having a Coca-Cola when Eric from Boston caught up to me, said, "Where you been, Cooper?" Eric's this big old redheaded fellow, talks like he's fixing to crack you over the head with something heavy. And he was there that day of the fire, the day I cut out with eight hundred dollars' worth of hardware in the back of my truck. I thought he might be trying to razz me, so I just nodded at him.

"Been around," I said.

"Around, huh?" said Eric. "Well how's she hanging?"

"Not too good, if you're asking."

"Yeah," he said. His eyes kind of moved over the room. "I mean obviously. Sorry, Shelley."

We stood there a while, talking like you do at a funeral, mentioning everything but the reason you're there. The weather, George Bush, I don't know. Eric's crazy for cars, he'll set there and chew your ear off about a car if you let him. He told me about the suspension wanted replacing in his vehicle, which is a 1965 Stingray he's trying to fix up like new. I told him about my truck, and how I wrecked the thing in Oklahoma, and when he wondered what I'd been doing in Oklahoma, I told him I'd been working for a man out there.

And Eric tilted his chin up, give me a look.

"So that's where you've been," he said. "You don't work for Jake anymore?"

And it's like I said, I thought Eric must be trying to razz me, but when I studied his face I knew better. So it hit me that Jake Lundeen never told anybody about that air compressor. Him and me and Mike Corliss are maybe the only ones knew why it had went missing for two months. And May, I suppose. You'd think I'd feel better, but I was just more ashamed. I looked crossed the room at Jake Lundeen, he was off talking to my sister, his hand on her shoulder, and I thought to myself, Lord mercy, I've got to get out of here.

But no sooner am I headed for the door than I feel a hand give my shoulder a little squeeze. I turn and there's the minister, holding his palm out to me.

"Mr. Cooper?" he says.

I just nod, shake his hand.

"Well I've heard an awful lot about you," he says.

"That right?"

"Your sister thinks you pretty much shot the moon." He had something on his face that was kind of like a smile. "She's come to visit me quite often in these past months. Just to talk."

I nod. I can't think of what to say, so I thank him for the sermon. But when he just looks embarrassed, I like him more.

"Thanks," he says. "Truth is, there isn't much to say, things like this. Sometimes a thing is too ugly to fit words to. You see what I mean?"

Yeah, I tell him, I know what he means.

"Still I think it helps. To be together, in His house. Maybe it isn't the place, exactly, but the I-don't-know-what. The community. It helps to know we are loved. I don't pretend it takes away our pain, but I believe it reminds us what He teaches, which is that with love we are bigger than our pain."

"Sure," I say. "I get you. Yeah."

And he is quiet, the way somebody will get quiet when he is waiting for you to tell him what's on your mind. It is the same quiet I heard when Mrs. Gamliel dropped me off at the church. Like hell am I going to say.

"We need each other," he tells me. "Times like this, more than ever. And May, she needs you now, too. The clothes and the other things, the medical bills, these are Christian things you've done for her. But now she needs generosity of spirit—"

I open my mouth to explain he's got the wrong Cooper. Instead, I tell him, "Yes, I can see that."

"You come too sometime," he says. "Door's always open."

"I know it is."

"Bring your wife," says the minister. "And your daughters."

I went to her after I'd spoke with the minister. I went, even if I didn't have much to say except I was sorry about it. You try finding the words. She was about half-rot with heartache, couldn't hardly stand. I don't remember what I told her, it's all kind of blurred up now. I remember I was standing beside her and she had her face buried in my neck, just the way a child will do.

Sorry, May, I think I said. I'm sorry. And when she let me go I went to find our brother.

Through a great big sliding door you could see the churchyard, and past that the plain before the mountains. If it'd been a clear day, I guess you might've made out Longs Peak and the little tufty hill they call the Haystack. But with the clouds so thick it was just a great grayness in the west. Clayton was standing, staring out the glass, watching the storm come on.

If you asked me what I walked over to him for, I don't believe I'd have an answer for you. It wasn't to apologize, I don't think, unless I'm wrong about that. Unless all I'm telling you here is that I did my brother dirty and I'm sorry for it.

"Go away, Shelley. Mercy, just go away."

But I didn't go away from him, I don't know why, exactly. Must've been some kind of death wish.

"I guess you still don't believe me," I told him. "I guess you think I stole it."

"Well it's gone, anyway," he said. "Isn't it?"

I took a second answering him, that ten grand setting heavy in the pockets of the jacket.

"Isn't it?" he said. Still he hadn't turned from the glass door.

"It isn't gone," I said. "Some junkie whore in Houston's got it."

He stood looking out the window, taking in that wide view of nothing.

"Well don't act like you're some angel in all this. Fifty grand's in that suitcase, and my cut's not even three? That makes an awful lot of profit for you, big brother."

And that was when he looked at me, when I saw his eyes taking in what Candy had done to my face. I saw honest-to-God worry in them eyes, too, and yet he said, "Profit? Profit?" Like he couldn't believe his ears. "Do you know what all this run me, Shelley? The doctors and the tests and more doctors to tell you the first doctors was wrong? Fifty grand, that'd barely cover it."

And that's when I seen Nancy. I remember she stood over on the far side of the hall, just watching us. A face old as the world. Maybe I only imagined her hand set to shaking when she put it up to her mouth.

And it would've been easy to tell my brother I was sorry for what all I'd done. The more I think of it, the more I'm sure that's what I meant to say: Forgive me.

"Here's the truth," I told him instead. "This junkie whore, I shouldn't have had her in the room with me, but I did. This junkie, she crack me with a bottle and bust my jaw and then she run off with your money. That's the truth."

Well Clayton just shook his head:

"Somebody run off with that money," he said. "And you just happen to show up in a brand-new suit."

When I walk outside, the storm's coming in thick, and it's so cold that the snow freezes fast to the sidewalk just soon as it falls. And in my fine shoes, I move slow and screw-footed as an old man, first down one block and then another, onto Main Street. And there it is, right at the corner of Main and Fourteenth, the Haystack Mountain Bar.

When you name a thing, you're just telling lies about it. A day like this, snow thick enough to blind you, you can't even see Haystack Mountain. And this is what I'm thinking about when I come up to the bar in the corpse's shoes and hear a voice calling my name. And though the music's on pretty loud, I believe I'd recognize Michael Corliss's voice in a howling gale.

Mike is setting over in a booth, the far side of the room. He's got a shot in front of him and two bottles of beer, one empty and the other half-empty. I guess he must've cut out as soon as the ministration ended, slipped out the back door maybe. Anyway, the bottles and the look in his eyes tells me that Mike has been at it for a while.

Also, he seems to have been having himself a cry. And it's not that I fault Mike for it, it's that he doesn't seem quite like himself somehow. His lips are drawed in and very pale, and his eyes all dazed and mean-looking. I think of his father. I think about how a taste for liquor will run in some families like blue eyes or red hair. I think about my sister, and I am afraid.

"You need one?" I call. I don't know why I've asked, I can see a drink is about the last thing Mike needs right now.

Rosa, that's the barmaid works there, come back from the kitchen.

"Hell happened to you?" is what she wants to know, but I won't explain now. I order two Coors. When she sets them down on the mahogany, I open my wallet and show her it's empty.

"I guess you spent it all on that suit," she says, lifting her lip.

"You can't give it to me on credit?"

207

"I could," she says. "Or I could just put it on Mike's tab."

Well usually I wouldn't abide such a thing, but then I remember I'm fixing to give my best friend Mike near ten grand.

I nod at her: "That's fine."

I take up the beers and walk over to Mike, trying to think of what I'm going to say to him. By the time I pull up to the table and set his beer down, I still don't have any real clear idea, so I don't say anything.

"What the hell," he says, and then he finishes the last of his beer in two quick gulps and picks up the beer I've just brought him.

"It ain't going anywhere," I tell him. "What's the hurry, exactly?" And then, when he doesn't answer, I ask him, "You going back, or what?"

"Back where?"

"Where you think."

"I don't know. No."

"I believe May would want you to come back there with me directly we finish these."

"What May would want."

"Yes."

"What you would want."

"Sure. It's what I would want, too."

"Boy, Shelley," he says. "You're like a. I don't know what you're like."

"Me, neither," I say.

"I take that back. You're a queer one."

"You about hit the nail on the head, Mike," I tell him. "What do you want me to say about it?"

"Nothing. Don't say anything. Just if you please get your ass out of here."

So I make to stand up: "Okay. Let's hit the trail, cowboy."

Mike doesn't move, though, and maybe I never expected him to.

"I guess you don't get it," he says. "That's the whole point here. What you think I left that church for, the first place."

I set down again. I tell him, "Easy, Mike."

And he says, "Easy, Mike." He gives me a look like he might like to knock me dead. "I'm finishing this beer and when I do it I'm going to have another. Or else I won't. First I'm going to ask you a simple question, Shelley: What the hell is wrong with you?"

And the bar seems like to grow dark, and I am a little sick to my stomach. But Mike isn't finished yet.

"Never mind," he says. "Don't answer that, don't even try it. About everybody in the world knows what the matter is but you."

And even now I can't be angry with him. I say, "You're suffering. You don't mean to talk this way. But don't think I'm going to set here and take it. I won't do that."

And he calls my bluff: "Then don't," he says. "Then get your lying, thieving, cocksucking ass out of here."

Well I wish I had went then. Probably you figured. But I didn't. The two of us set there thinking the whole thing over. You sort of wanted to explain to the fellow that you'd come there for him, that nothing much else in the world mattered to you. But that's not what I said. I told him, fine, I'd leave him to set and feel sorry for himself.

"Before I go," I told him, "I've got something to give to you."

And I reached into the pocket of the suit jacket and took out the first stack of cash and set it on the table, and then I reached into the other pocket and took out the second stack and set it on the table.

"This here is ten thousand dollars," I said, "it's for the funeral and for medical bills. I guess you know I wish it was more. Well I do. I wish it was a whole lot more."

But I quit off talking cause Mike had his head in his hands and his shoulders drawed up like the heckles on a dog. At first I thought he was crying again, but when he looked up at me I saw that wasn't it. That wasn't it at all.

"Jesus, Shelley," he said. "Get that out of my sight."

I thought he might mean account of we were in public. But Rosa had went in the back again and we were the only two in the bar now.

"Get it out of my sight. My God. What is wrong with you? What in the hell is wrong with you?"

"I understand you're proud," I said. "But don't let pride keep you from taking this. I'm like a brother to you. More than a brother, some ways."

"Brothers? Brothers, Jesus."

I held my peace, deciding this was the kind of conversation where a fellow might say something he didn't mean. Matter of fact, I reckoned Mike had already said a thing or two he was liable to regret later on. I was doing my best to steel myself, bear up for what come next, but there wasn't anything could've got me ready:

"It was you," he said.

"Me what?"

"It was you started that fire."

I just blinked at him, couldn't find my voice at first. When I did, I talked foolish: "You've drunk yourself crazy," I said. "I was standing right next to you when that mountain went up. I wasn't but a hundred feet away from you."

"Not that fire," he said. "Starbuck's truck. It was you."

"The hell are you talking about?" I said, pretending to think. "Starbuck? Laughton Starbuck?"

"My God," he said, shaking his head. "My God, my God."

When he didn't say more, I told him, "I believe I'm right. I believe you've drunk yourself crazy after all."

"Fine," he said. "I drunk myself crazy. But it's true and you know it's true. I don't know why you did it. I never knew why and I still don't, except you didn't like to see me with your sister. You didn't like seeing me with anybody but you."

I just looked at him for a second. I couldn't believe the ugliness inside of him, and in an ugly flash it hit me where it must come from.

"You've been talking to Clayton," I said. "Clay's filled you up with this shit."

But Mike never answered me, exactly.

"Just talk square to me" is what he told me instead. "I'd like you to talk square, just this one time in your life. You torched that truck and you let everyone think I done it."

"You're a fool."

"And you're worse than that," he said. "You sold your own brother out to the Law. It was you told them where to find it."

"Find what?" I said, the words burning like hot coals in my mouth. "His dope? Jesus, you're out of your mind."

"You're a sickness, Shelley," he said then. "You're a kind of disease. You make my fucking skin crawl."

"You're drunk," I told him. "You're just drunk."

"Sure, I'm a little drunk. But I'm not as drunk as you might like to think I am. I'm sick of you, that's all. I'm sick to death of you and sick to death of pretending I ain't."

After a very long while he said, "You've got nothing to say?"

"What do you want me to say?"

"I don't care," he said. "Just as long as you hear me. And you'd better hear me on this, too: me and May are leaving."

"The hell are you talking about?"

"I'm talking about we're going," he said, "and this time you'd better not follow us."

I couldn't believe what he was saying: "Follow you?" I said. "You're the one told me come out here, the first place. You're the one got me work on Lundeen's crew."

"She made me do it. Her and Clay."

And I guess my face told him something I never wanted it to.

"That's right," he said. "Clayton. You wouldn't be here, it wasn't for him."

I thought about that. It was queer news, but then I figured the snakes must like to keep the rats close by. Never mind that, I thought.

"Well you're going. And do what?"

"What's it to you?"

"Nothing. And what about your house?" I said. "What about that?"

"We're selling."

"To who?"

"Somebody. Who to hell cares. I'd just about give it to them. But I can't stay here anymore."

Well it was just ugly enough to be true. I wanted to ask him what May thought of all that, leaving her kin behind, but by then I could see she didn't matter. So I just shrugged, trying to show Michael Corliss he could do what he liked, it wasn't going to bother me any. But something was coming undone, breaking apart. Mike was sore—about the air compressor, for one thing, and me being gone when Layla passed—but he was something else besides sore. He'd come to hate me. And I guess I don't see any reason not to tell you here, I don't see any reason not to tell you my heart was breaking. I loved him very much. Maybe I still do.

"Well I guess I'll leave you alone then," I said. "I guess I'll leave you here, since that's what you seem to want."

And I stood up cause I thought he might try to keep me from going. And that's the part, when I think about all this now, I'm most shamed of.

XIV

First week of February, I run into Diego, that's my neighbor. Diego's an all right guy, but a little nosy, and he wanted to know where all I'd been lately, and I told him about the accident down in Oklahoma. Dang, said Diego. And then he said he was fixing to sell his truck. I asked him how much did he want for it and he said he couldn't take less than three, account of he'd just put new shocks in.

"Well I don't intend to take it off-road," I said. "I don't care how good the shocks are."

And Diego kind of scratched the back of his head: "Come look at it," he said.

So I followed him down to the apartment lot and he showed me his vehicle, and I took a good look at the truck. And I seen sure enough he'd put new shocks in, and the engine was good, too, and if he was trying to sell it for any less than four grand then either he was desperate or he'd lost his mind.

"I'll give you two," I told him. "Looks like there's some body work needs done."

I was talking about his taillight. The right one'd been shucked out, and now I hooked my finger over the cutting edge of yellow plastic.

"Well it ain't even four years old," he said. "I can't do less than three."

And I told him, "Twenty-five."

And after a while he said, "Fuck it."

Next day I brung him $2,500 in an envelope and we gone down to the county tax office and he give me the title and bill of sale and the government took another bite out of my ass. When I got home from the tax office, May was standing there.

It was winter yet, but a hot, quick wind was blowing in from the west. A chinook, they call that. She was standing outside my door, waiting, this look on her face like did you really figure I'd just let you be? Her hair was cut real short now, short as a boy's, and it looked darker, too. Her arms were folded over her chest in a way that put me in mind of somebody. Maybe it was Momma, but I don't think so. She didn't say anything for a minute, and then she turned her face against that hot wind and held her hand against the sun.

"You asshole," she said.

"Well come on in."

I opened the door and we stood there a while just inside. May was quiet, taking in the dishes along the counters, the trails I'd cut through the mess on the floor. You ever notice a place never looks as dirty as in the light of an evening?

May said, "Your fridge."

I said, "What about it?"

"What have you got in it?"

She stepped past a wadded-up pair of blue jeans and a paper bag full of beer cans and beer tabs and microwavable supper containers toppled over on its side. She come to the fridge, eyeing it for a second before she opened the door.

"Okay, Shell," she said. "What's going on in here?"

"What?" I asked her. "You mean the Chinese?"

"Is that what it is?"

I said the Chinese food was the oldest of what all was in there.

She shut the door and asked was I fixing to eat it, and when I didn't answer May shook her head and begun to open the kitchen cabinets one by one until she found a package of Hefty bags I couldn't rightly remember buying.

It had been a long time since I'd cleaned up the place any, it was just I'd been busy at work. That's what I tried to get May to understand while we tidied up the kitchen and the den: I was working pretty much full-time at the 7-Eleven, account of we were short-staffed lately, this guy Robbie had been skivving right out of the till.

"Well I'm glad you're working," she said, but she didn't say why this was so.

"They're talking about making me the night manager," I said. "Pay raise, I don't know what all."

"You've put on a little weight, too," she said. "That's good."

But I knew the truth, which was that I'd thickened out, especially round my midsection. I didn't much care for it.

"Doesn't beat working outside, though. Not even close."

I thought for a minute about that gig up Left Hand Road. The sun on my back, that jack-pine smell. Then that fire coming to take everything. I thought about Mike.

"So I guess you all haven't sold your place yet?"

I had waited some time to ask. I wasn't sure what all Mike had told her about that afternoon in the Haystack.

"Oh, no," she said. "Took about a New York minute to sell. Working it all out with the bank right now."

217

"That's good," I told her. "I imagine you'll be glad to be quit of all this."

"All what?"

I had been stooped down cleaning the coffee table, but now I straightened up and looked at her: "Colorado, I mean. What all has happened."

"What do you mean, quit?" she said. "I'm not going anywhere."

So, I thought to myself, they're staying. Funny thing was, somehow I wasn't all that glad to hear it. Sometime, I'd come to want him to leave.

"So where you and Mike staying, if you've sold the house?"

May just shrugged. She said Mike had left already, that he was out in Phoenix, where Eric had got him a job on his cousin's framing crew. And yet all this was not quite square in my head. I couldn't quite get my mind around it.

"And what about you? You'll go out there after a while, I guess?"

May's voice went all hissy: "I just said I'm staying."

So that's that, I figured: Mike done cut out.

You wait long enough, everybody'll let you down. And had I been a younger man, I might've got angry. I might've wanted to put my hands round his goddamned neck for leaving my sister in the lurch. But them days are past me now.

Me and May cleaned like that for a while, until after the sun had went down and even the porcelain in the bathroom sink seemed to shine. We talked some, not about anything special. I don't believe anybody even mentioned Layla. Before long, May said she'd had enough, she was fixing to get back home.

I did a turn, looking everything over. The place had never looked so good.

"Thanks, May," I told her, and it was like she'd been waiting for me to say it: her cheeks went all red and her eyes took on a mean-looking fire when she narrowed them on me.

"I don't know what I did it for, that's the truth," she said. "I haven't seen you since I don't know when."

But I knew how long it had been, and I guess she knew it, too.

"I'm sorry," I said, cause by now May was blubbering like a little baby. "I'm sorry for everything, May."

And I was sorry, too, it wasn't any lie: I felt awful.

"You're about up to your neck in shit, little brother," she said, but I didn't need her telling me. I had quit dreaming about hell. Them days, all I dreamed about was the dead. They come floating up to me from the bottom. And for a crazy second, I wondered was that what she come here to tell me? Repent, Shelley. But all that's between me and you, and Houston.

She said, "When are you going to see Clayton?"

I felt the hair drawing up on my neck.

"How do you mean?"

But May didn't back down any. She said, "You need to figure out how you're going to pay him back, and soon."

"Pay him back for what? I told him I couldn't help losing it. Somebody robbed me."

"Which means you robbed him," she said.

Which was the plain truth, and I knew it.

"How you think he's going to feed those girls?" She was nearly shouting now. "You ever think of that?"

Yes, I told her. Of course I'd thought of it. I thought of it every day. My whole brain was full of things I couldn't quit thinking about. Just then I was thinking how I wasn't ever going to pay him back on a gas clerk's wages. Just then I was thinking of Jake

Lundeen in his trailer, the day I give him back that air compressor. Just then I was thinking: Repent.

Still, there was a piece of me figured it was all a bunch of crying over spilled mash, wasn't it? The money was gone. Besides that, in a way it had been mine to lose. And I guess May must've saw what was in my mind cause she said:

"Hell with it."

But May's words must've worked on me, even if I didn't quite know it. That same week she come to my place, I went to see Lundeen. He didn't look all that glad to see me, but then he didn't look sore, either. I asked did he think he could put me back on the crew and he give a quiet kind of laugh and said:

"I'm not sure, Shell, but I sort of don't think so."

And I nodded and said I was sorry to bother him and turned to walk out.

"You in trouble, Shell?" he called, when I was just about to the door.

I saw no reason to lie: "Yeah," I said, "I'm in a little trouble."

"How much trouble?" Jake Lundeen wanted to know.

"About fifty thousand dollars' worth," I said.

He just watched me for a while, half smiling until he realized I was dead serious. Then he said he'd see what he could manage. I turned for the door again, and his voice stopped me.

"You know, Shell," he called, "the two of us've probably got more in common than you think."

I turned and looked at him. He'd stood up out of his chair, though he made no move to step round the desk.

"I'm saying, probably we've got more in common than you know."

And I thought about where he kept that book of checks, three to a page. And I thought about the air compressor, and that pawn clerk, and how Carter Landreau's eyes looked when I fit my hands round his neck, kind of misty and red. And I said aloud what I was thinking, which was:

"No offense, Mr. Lundeen. But I don't think we've got much in common at all."

So let me tell you what happened and you can go ahead and decide. That night in Houston I set in my truck while the buzz and hum of that evil city run through my veins. I wanted to leave, soon as I could. And that's the funny thing, I almost never gone back that night—funny is not the word I want—I set there thinking to myself, The hell with it all. But when I felt the key in my pocket I knew I couldn't leave, and a chill went through me didn't have anything to do with the hard edge of cold on the air.

I was shivering by the time I pulled up out front of the Seaside, nervous even if it was quiet out, and the lights off. It was not quite morning yet, and them great big live oaks leaning up and over the cut of the roof like billowy black clouds.

I skittered like a rat crossed the parking lot, slinked through the gimpy hedge and round back of the bungalow, set there trying to get my courage up. And then, hunched so low I was nigh crawling, I slithered through the cars.

I don't know what I was thinking. I was thinking about the jangle of change in my pocket. I was thinking nobody better drive off with my truck. I was thinking that him who sows the wind reaps it. I jammed the key in the door and turned the lock and opened it wide. And God knows how many times I have thought to myself, If only it had been somebody else setting on that bed with the

221

toolbox open on the floor and the panel off the back of the TV. If only it had been Clint, or Mrs. Landreau, or that ten-dollar whore. But there on the bed was this fine-looking man with eyes like the sky when there's nothing going to happen. He's setting there, fifteen large right there next to him.

"Well sure now," he said. There was a smile in his voice, like us two were in on some joke. And when I didn't answer one way or the other, he went on, "Sure now. This why you didn't want to leave the room."

I started on Jake Lundeen's crew end of February, same week May and me moved into the place we live now, on the first floor of the Hover Place Apartments. It's a two-bedroom right next to Mrs. Gamliel's unit, which seemed to please her. When we'd hauled in all the furniture May had brung from her and Mike's place, Mrs. Gamliel said, "It is good to have a woman's touch. Shelley, don't you agree?"

The recliner was gone now, wasn't enough room for it. The stringy couch I'd found in the alley behind the Haystack was gone, too, along with that fold-up card table where I'd used to take my meals. That night the three of us ate on Lij Cooper's old red Formica table. Supper wasn't anything much—chicken and potato salad, green beans from a can—but Mrs. Gamliel set to moaning and rubbing her belly like it was the best meal she'd ever had.

"Delicious," she told May.

And May said, "Thank you, Mrs. Gamliel, but it's nothing special."

And Mrs. Gamliel said, "Please, call me Luisa."

Them two were what you'd call fast friends, I guess, which didn't surprise me any: they were both of them real good and kindhearted women whose bad luck run longer than an interstate. I remember that after a while Mrs. Gamliel commenced talking about the day I come to ask about the apartment-for-rent sign. She told how I stood out in the cold in just a sweat shirt, and my teeth chattering when I asked her, Excuse me, ma'am, is the apartment still available?

And May turned her eyes on me: "Don't let him fool you, Luisa," she said. "Don't let him fool you for a second."

And again I was standing in that room, going, "That money isn't mine, Mr. Landreau."

Carter was shaking his head. He had changed out of the bathrobe by then, now he wore khaki slacks and a light blue jacket over a plain white tee shirt: STAFFORD PETROLEUM, read the decal over the breast pocket of the jacket. He asked, "What'd you hide it here for?" And still he spoke in that voice like the two of us are waiting on a punch line. And a piece of me must've wanted to set laughing with him over the strangeness of the thing: a man hides his brother's money in another man's TV set. A piece of me must've saw the humor. It can't be the only thought in my mind was whether Carter Landreau still had the Luger on him. I figured he must have it tucked in his waistband, at the small of his back, the way his brother-in-law had done.

"Mr. Landreau," I told him, "I'm asking you to believe me. I'll be in a jackpot without that fifteen grand."

He seemed to think about coming to his feet. Maybe he thought to take a run at me, or a swing. He had set that hook on his gimpy arm again, and it flashed sharp as a hay grappler. Maybe he thought of the money him and his wife had yet on the mortgage, the one the disability wouldn't quite cover.

He asked, "Well if your money's hid here, what'd your friend run off with?"

"Friend?" I said. "You're the only friend I've got here."

223

"Candy," he said, and now Carter smiled. It was that smile you give somebody when you're happy not to stand in his shoes.

"My suitcase," I told him, cause I couldn't explain what foolishness had brought us here together. That I'd took an idiot notion in my head. That when I looked around for some place to put my new cut, my eye had caught on a busted TV set.

"Seems to me you're already in a jackpot, Mr. Corliss."

"I am," I said. "I mean an even bigger jackpot."

And still he was smiling, smiling in such a way that I knew he had the Luger somewhere, that probably it was tucked in the waistband of his slacks like I'd thought it must be. And it occurred to me again how everybody'll let you down, you wait long enough. It had took Carter Landreau one solitary day.

"I can't explain it to you," I said.

"Try," he said. "Try it, bud." And I knew from the look in his eye, he wanted me to beg.

So I did.

"Carter," I said, "I'm begging you."

I took a step farther into the room and he seemed to set straighter on the bed. I guess a fright had run through him, but still he didn't make no move to stand, or to grab behind him.

And for the second time in as many days, my eye caught on the toolbox. The bone-white handle of the plumber's mallet. I was very calm somehow when I saw it. I wonder now if I'd thought it all out. I wonder if I guessed all the things his body meant to tell me. All the things mine meant to answer. I wonder did I think, Best get it over with.

"I've got to get on the road, Mr. Landreau," I told him. "And I need that fifteen grand."

"Well hold on," he said, all easy-breezy. "What d'you think the police would have to say about this? What d'you think they'd do if I called and explained who put two bullet holes in my wall?"

And I nodded, half-sure he was a good man again. Somehow I could abide the Law easier than the other thing. What was the other thing? It was that hunger I could smell on the air, a sort of hot emptiness.

"Surprised you ain't called them yet," I told him. "If you think it's the right thing to do, then you ought to call the police."

But Carter Landreau wanted that money, and he wanted me to let him take it.

"Call the Law? They'll take you to jail."

"They will."

"You'd like that?"

"I wouldn't like it, no. But I wouldn't hold it against you."

He looked at me a moment, wagging his head, and with a smile on his face that made you want to smash his brains in. And the plumber mallet calling out to me in Lij's voice, going: God help him, God help him if he crosses you.

"You're crazy," said Carter Landreau. "I wouldn't want the police here, I was you. What all you've got up to in this place . . ."

"I haven't bothered anybody," I told him. "No one."

And now I was standing near enough I could reach and grab the plumber's mallet and draw it up over my head and down upon him. It was going to be almost easy, except that Carter Landreau wanted to break my heart first.

"We're keeping all this a secret," he said, and drew the Luger out from where he had it tucked in his slacks, at the small of his back, and he set it between his knees to try to work the action. But it's like I told you, it'd be awful hard to shoot a Luger with one hand. I watched him trying to work the toggle, gripping the barrel tight between his knees. It went through my mind like wildfire: Be quick, Shell, if you're doing it.

And somebody shouts, Fire! And so we start loading everything up: skill saws and quick saws and pneumatics and drills. A pair of air compressors, an old one and a new one, and without quite thinking to do it you are setting the new one in the back of your truck. It's that old voice that's told you to do it, that old snake hissing, except now you know better. Now you know that voice was the only thing ever belonged to you. You are standing with the pawn ticket in your hand, grim and quiet as black-winged death himself.

And so it was I walked quick to Carter with the plumber's mallet, I drawed red on his forehead with it. The pistol slipped from in between his knees, he held his good hand to bare bone. After that I put my hands round his throat, and I choked him dry. I remember that hook coming soft, soft, soft against my jacket.

Not that I figure being sorry makes a thing better. Love your neighbor is what they tell you, never mentioning that loving your neighbor means hating him a little, too. And here's the wages of it: his eyes gone a misty red, and the bruises like black cobwebs round his lily-white neck. I bent down, I picked up the Luger.

When Mrs. Gamliel left that night, me and May did the dishes while I thought it all over. I had been doing that for going on two months: trying to think of the right thing to do. My head hurt from thinking about it so long, and so I turned to May, said: "Just wait here a minute." I walked back to my room, where the moving boxes was stacked in one corner. I took the top box down and worked it open and set it all on the bed: the brown paper bag from the liquor store in Houston, and inside the bag was a King James Bible, and tucked inside the

Bible was an envelope. I peeled off the packing tape I'd used to seal the envelope, and then I took out the seven and a half grand cash I had in there. After that I went back to May at the sink, saying:

"I need you to give this to Clayton."

But already she was shaking her head, going, "No, nope, no way." And we stood there in the kitchen, me kind of waving the bills at her and May telling me, "Not a chance, little brother, you'd better do your own dirty work."

Truth is, I don't believe May noticed a difference in me after I come back from Houston, seeing as she had her own troubles. I could hear her crying sometimes to herself in the next room, them walls were like wax paper. Neither was I sleeping too good. If I did, I dreamed I was awake. I dreamed I was driving to the work site, Lundeen's contract out in Golden. Big old houses with frames that chew up whole hours, whole days. Big old piñon pine all gathered around them lots like a noose. Like a fuse. And in the dream that wasn't a dream, there come this great wall of hellfire, and I burned.

Now that Mike Corliss and Eric from Phoenix had lit out for the traces, Tiny Tim was foreman on the crew. It was him and me, and Hector and Luis, and we managed all right for a while, and then Jake Lundeen hired a whole bunch of new blood, and them boys were just green as grass.

Ryan was the worst of them, a great big dumb ox of a dude. Not much taller than me but near twice as wide in the shoulders, with a smile straight as a razor and dumb as a bag of bricks. Ryan Blaylock from Okfuskee, Oklahoma. We called him Okie until the day Tiny Tim had him cutting fireproofing. When Tiny Tim give

him an earful about what a piss-poor job he done, Ryan held up
the skill saw, said, "I'm all thumbs with this thing!"

After that, he was Thumbs.

And even in that bone-cutting cold, Thumbs liked to strip off
his shirt and work, muscles swaying and tightening in his chest
and arms. And once I called up to him: "You working on your
tan, Miss America?" And Thumbs give me that dumb-as-bricks
smile, his eyes skittering away from mine, his face so red you'd
have thought he was choking.

First Friday in March, payday, I took two weeks' wages, plus
what was left of the cash from the security box and drove up to
my brother's spread. I drove past Nederland, past the scraggly
creek that'd be a great river when the thaw come. The road cork-
screwed up, and then come the gate and Clayton's lane. Just like
I'd done in the winter, I parked and got out and walked. And it
was that same blue as in the winter, except it was dusk and not
dawn this time.

I moved slow, my boots crunching in the banked snow. I don't
know exactly what I was thinking of—nothing, maybe. But underneath of nothing was the ice-cold certainty that I must be sorry.
I was bringing this money to Clayton. Which meant I thought it
was his. Which meant I was sorry for taking it. Which meant I was
sorry for the man I'd killed getting it back.

You can quit a job and you can quit drinking and you can quit
smoking and you can quit thieving or robbing banks or growing
dope. But you can't ever quit being a murderer. That's on you like
a birthmark. And I believe I've had my mark long as I've known
Michael Edward Corliss. Wanting him, I mean, knowing better
than to do it. Wanting him anyway.

The trailer come into view past the roll and dive of them great big peaks. I sometimes wonder, do all the mountains have names? Every rise in the earth?

And I saw it all laid out before me. I saw me opening the door and reaching down for the plumber's mallet. I saw me holding out the envelope and explaining this was all I had until next payday. I saw all of it.

But here's what happened: when I heard Misty howling inside, I opened the screen door and set the envelope up against the weatherproofing. Then I turned and run back to my truck. All that ice, it's a miracle I didn't break my neck.

Supper that night, I had a queer feeling. I don't know quite how to explain it to you. May told about her shift at the nursing home in Boulder, and Mrs. Gamliel told about a busted shower head in apartment 2F, but while they talked I could feel their eyes cutting over to me, like as if they knew how come I'd lingered at work nigh two hours later than usual. Like as if they knew where I'd been, and why. Like as if they could smell Carter's blood, drying yet on my jacket.

When the phone rang, it was May who stood and answered it. It was Clayton calling, I knew it from the way she said, "Oh, it's you again." For a while them two traded wisecracks, and then May turned to me:

"Your brother," she said, in a phony queen of England voice, "desires a word."

"I'm eating supper," I pointed out.

"Shelley," she said. "Come on now."

So I went, I took up the phone.

"I guess you come up to the house," said Clayton's voice.

I didn't answer for a minute, just listened to him breathing.

"I hope I don't have to tell you, you're about forty grand short."

A beat passed before I could answer: "I don't get paid for another two weeks."

He was quiet. Considering. Deciding did he like this arrangement or not.

"So you're on some kind of installment plan?" he said. "That what this shit is?"

I told him, "Something like that."

"Something like that," he said. "The hell does that mean?"

At the table, May and Mrs. Gamliel set very quiet. Not even pretending not to listen.

"Look," I said, "we've got company. Lady owns the place come to supper."

Another beat.

"Well I just called to tell you something," he said.

"I'm waiting for it."

"Next time, just come in. Okay? Say hello to Nancy and the girls, is what I'm saying."

I wondered could I smell a trap. I wondered is he forgiving me. I wondered was there any such thing as forgiveness. Still I don't know. After a while I said, "All right."

"Have a bite to eat, even."

"Yeah, okay."

"Nance made chili tonight," he said.

And I said, "It's the weather for it."

And he said, "That's for sure: April in the mountains, it's like December in the hills."

And when I got off the phone, May and Mrs. Gamliel were still setting there, quiet, and then Mrs. Gamliel said, "This was your brother? Clayton?"

"Yes," I said, "the same one."

"The big fellow?"

"Yes," I said, "him."

"Such a nice man," said Mrs. Gamliel.

And May kind of chuckled at that. Said, "Don't let him fool you, not for a second."

You miss the signs, I guess, or anyway you can't read them until it's too late. I left Houston in a goddamned hurry, drove those same miles I'd covered hardly a day earlier. It couldn't have been noon by the time I saw that billboard outside Dallas, them two boys in hard hats, smiling and shaking hands:

A BRIGHTER FUTURE TOGETHER:
STAFFORD PETROLEUM IS NOW
RUBICON OIL AND GAS.

I kept north on I-35, on through Dallas, missed the turnoff for Amarillo and kept on through north Texas, where there wasn't anything but the wind, and the land dry as bone, and ice in the air. South Oklahoma, I wondered maybe they've found Carter Landreau, maybe every highway patrol from Louisiana to New Mexico is hunting a rusty old F-150 with Missouri plates.

I can't remember what this little bullshit town was called, maybe it has no name. Anyway that's where I ditched it, half a mile or so outside the limits, off on this country road with a view of more sandy plains and a blue kind of crust of river. Clouds that looked nickel-plated churning in from the west to turn a yellow sun paper-white.

Not that you paid any mind to it. I pulled off half a mile from nowhere. I ripped out the VIN numbers and unscrewed the plates with the pliers I had in the glove box. I tucked the Luger under the driver's seat, same as it ever was. Then I set to walking.

Didn't stop until I come up on one of them places that's half gas station and half café. That's where I crossed this waitress. This big old blonde and sway-butted thing. I ordered eggs and taters and bacon I never worked up the appetite to eat. When she come with my check I asked her where could I catch a west-bound bus.

"There is no westbound," she said. And the way she watched me made me sure of it, sure she was fixing to call the Law on me.

Next morning we set to laying the foundation and digging the postholes. And that day and the next kind of slanting by, and the third morning Thumbs come up to me with his hands held out in front of him and blood running down his arms.

"The hell happened?"

"I was mixing concrete," he said. "For the postholes."

And I said, "With your bare hands?"

And he went red in the face.

I was the one drove him to the hospital. Highway 93, which cuts right past Rocky Flats, where they make the nukes. And while I drove, Thumbs told tall tales about mutant refugees from that place. Five-legged deer, jackrabbits with fangs like bats, turtles with fins like lake trout. And I smiled, thinking of Mike Corliss: Bullshit, I told Thumbs. I don't know why, maybe I was just trying to razz him a little. But Thumbs just smiled back.

"Well, sure," he said, "I never saw it. But my cousin works for the BLM, he says . . ."

He talked on and on that way until I pulled up out front of the hospital. He was still talking when he opened the door and got out, not trying all that hard to keep the mess off the handle. You couldn't stay mad at the kid, though. I asked did he have a ride home, and he said sure, he'd call someone.

That was the last I seen of Thumbs. He didn't show up to work that next day, or the day after that. At first I figured it was his hands giving him trouble, cement poisoning's no fun. Then Thumbs missed one whole week, and I knew I'd never see him again.

Time seemed to run slower after that. Tiny Tim wasn't much of a foreman, and the grade was off besides, and one day the fire marshal drove up and did a slow lap around the development. And then he come up alongside of where me and Hector were taking the measurements for the postholes Thumbs'd been supposed to dig before he cut out.

Fire marshal said, "Who's the contractor on this bid?"

And me and Hector looked at each other and shrugged our shoulders. We couldn't remember his name, we said.

And the fire marshal said, "Well whose name is on your paycheck?"

And we said, "He pays us cash."

And he said, "I find that hard to believe."

And we just looked at him until he shook his head and raised his window and drove off again.

Two days later come payday.

I was getting out of my truck when Jake Lundeen opened wide the door to his trailer.

"Cooper," he said, "get your ass in here."

By now I had saw the red Crown Victoria parked in the gravel next Lundeen's Mark VII. Through its window I had made out the dispatch radio next the steering wheel. I knew it was the Law come hunting me up even before I ducked through the door and seen that long, tall man in his dark suit.

Funny thing was, it never occurred to me to run. I guess I was just too curious, wanted to see how he'd found me. The VIN numbers and the plates was gone, and Lij's Luger wasn't registered, and I didn't think it was likely somebody had hunted up that plumber's mallet, and even if they had—

And then I remembered that little speck of a town, the nickel-plated clouds, the waitress who had eyeballed me for a second before she answered. And the Law watching me just like she did. Like he didn't much like the look of me. He was dishwater blond, this fellow, with potholes in his face. In that suit, he looked about long and skinny as a rat snake.

"I'm going to ask you just once," Lundeen said, "and I want a straight answer."

"Yes," I said, "I understand."

"Did you take it?"

I just stood there, trying to decide what he must mean. Take it? Take the plumber's mallet? The security box? The key to room fourteen? It wasn't until right that very second I begun to look around some, and I seen Jake Lundeen's trailer was wrecked all to hell. That dream-catching thing and the hunk of flagstone had been knocked off the wall, same with that picture of Lundeen and his buddies in Vietnam. The frame busted. One window had been cracked and there was a great spray of glass crossed of the carpet. I could see one, two, three, four, five drops of blood breadcrumbing over to the steel shelf, the one where Jake Lundeen kept that book of checks. Three to a page. I don't know why, maybe it was just the stains on the floor, but I was thinking of that day Thumbs come to me with his hands out in front of him, and the blood running down his arms, and I was thinking, Son of a bitch.

I said, "You've been robbed, Mr. Lundeen."

And Lundeen said, "You don't say."

The Law cleared his throat then, introduced himself. I think he said his name was Lieutenant Stevens, but I can't remember and anyways it doesn't matter much. He said, "Do you know anything about this, Mr. Cooper?"

Hell no, I said. I sure didn't.

You work that job long enough, probably you can tell if a man is guilty just by looking him in the eyes. The Law's eyes were green as jade. Now he frowned, crossing my name off the list of prime suspects.

"You have any idea who might've done this?" the Law wanted to know. "One of your coworkers, for instance. Anybody who's been acting suspicious."

Then a door seemed like to shut inside of me.

"Suspicious how?"

"Suspicious—like, say, missing work?"

I pretended to think, even though RYAN BLAYLOCK was flashing in my mind in bright red letters. After a quiet while, I said, "Well I don't think so." And then after another quiet while, I said, "You sure it was somebody on the crew?"

And then Jake Lundeen chuffed like a horse, "Somebody breaks in here and all he takes is the checkbook and the petty cash? Yeah, Cooper, I'd say he works here."

They will find Thumbs someday, just like they will find me. Still I am thinking of that waitress in Oklahoma, the one who watched me for a second or two before she answered, "There is no westbound. It's just north to south come through here. To go west you've got to ride up to KC, get the westbound there."

Which I took as a kind of sign.

I paid with that twenty I'd never got round to giving to Candy. When the waitress brung me the change, she stood there eyeballing me a while longer.

"Car accident?" she wanted to know.

"Car accident," I told her.

And then I went out into the cold, a pillowcase tucked into my jacket, and I rolled a pair of quarters into the slot to call my ex. What happened after that, I already explained it to you.

That day after the Law come, I had to tell Clayton about the checkbook on account of me not paying what was due, I had to tell about Jake Lundeen getting robbed. But I could hear in my brother's voice, he didn't believe a word. I don't blame him, I wouldn't believe me, either.

Come Monday, Lundeen himself drove out to Golden in that Mark VII. He set for a while just watching. Then he called out to Tiny Tim:

"Where's the rookie?"

And Tiny Tim just shrugged. We all of us know how this kind of thing goes. Thumbs will come back in a week or two, and if he's smart he'll wear gloves so we don't see where the glass from Lundeen's window bit into his knuckles. We will work and we will work until the fire come in a hungry wave.

And after that? After the fire's nothing but ash and ember? That's when the lesson finally takes.

The author would like to thank his family. In no particular order: his mom and his sisters and his Roshni, as well as Adam and John Henri. And Phil. Also: Ed and Suehelen, Cindy and Paul, Kuba, Janet G., Janet E., Ann, Pam, KT, Gracia, Scott, Ricky, Hutch, Ramesh and Chirag. Also: Travis, Noa, Paul, Zack, Jane, Aaron, Rachel, Robyn, and their children and the people they love. Thanks to everybody who continues to celebrate John Lee's life. Special thanks to Ravi and Dottie, and to their parents.

The author would like to thank the guys on Eric's crew.

The author would like to thank the students and faculty at the University of Houston. He feels a special debt of gratitude to Roberto Tejada, Chitra Divakaruni, Robert Boswell, Alexander Parsons, and Martha Serpas. He feels so grateful for the friendship of Butch, Selena, Henk, Tavi, Danny, Allie and Jon, Rolater and Anderson, Thomas and Tati and the new Calder, Sammy boy, Will, Jon and Alana, Dana, Conor and Rachel, Becky and Ro and the new Hallman-Paula.

The author would like to thank the Johns Hopkins Writing Seminars. Thanks especially to Alice McDermott for her gifts of wisdom and humility. Thanks to Jean McGerry for vision. Thanks to his spiritual guru, Linda Gottlieb, without whose patient friendship this book probably wouldn't exist. Thanks to Thomas, Lauren, Angela, Maggie, Robyn, Ryan, Patrick, Liz, Caroline, Petrina and Ty, Eric, Court, Gabrielle, and, yes, Manuel.

Many thanks to the English department at Hamline University, and a special thanks to Michael Reynolds, David Mura, and Carolyn Holbrook, who helped the author decide not to drop out of college. Thank you to the Accountability Team, for keeping him accountable.

Many thanks to the editors who published excerpts of this novel as short stories: *New Ohio Review*'s David Wanczyk and *Cimarron Review*'s Toni Graham. This book is in no small part the product of two passionate and brilliant women: Emma Komlos-Hrobsky, who rescued the first chapter of this novel from *Tin House*'s slush pile and later acquired the novel from Katie Zanecchia, whose suggestions enriched the manuscript immeasurably. The author is really proud to count you both among his friends.

To Justin St. Germain, many thanks for reading, and for your wonderful book, and for many more to come.

Finally, the author would like to thank the guests at the Covenant House, especially those who attended the writers workshop on Tuesday evenings. Thanks to Sara Mirza and Elysia Garcia, who kept the fire burning brighter. May you all continue to burn bright.

It sucks that the author has lost touch with so many of the people on this incomplete list.

PHOTO © KATY TARTAKOFF

JP GRITTON's awards include a Cynthia Woods Mitchell fellowship, a Disquiet fellowship, and the Donald Barthelme prize in fiction. His stories have appeared or are forthcoming in *Black Warrior Review, Greensboro Review, New Ohio Review, Southwest Review, Tin House*, and elsewhere. His translations of the fiction of Brazilian writer Cidinha da Silva have appeared in *InTranslation*. *Wyoming* is his first novel.